THE TWO SHOEMAKERS

THE TWO SHOEMAKERS

BY

HANNAH MORE

MINNEAPOLIS
2010

Published by Curiosmith.
P. O. Box 390293, Minneapolis, Minnesota, 55439.
Internet: curiosmith.com.
E-mail: shopkeeper@curiosmith.com.

Previously printed by Hazard, Marshall and White in 1795.

Scripture quotations are from the *Holy Bible*, King James Version.

All boldface footnotes are from previous editions.
All other footnotes are from the publisher.

ISBN 9781935626053

CONTENTS

PART I

JACK BROWN AND JAMES STOCK

JACK BROWN and James Stock were two lads apprenticed, at nearly the same time, to Mr. Williams, a shoemaker in a small town in Oxfordshire; they were pretty near the same age, but of very different characters and dispositions.

Brown was eldest son to a farmer in good circumstances, who gave the usual apprentice fee with him. Being a wild, giddy boy, whom his father could not well manage or instruct in farming, he thought it better to send him out to learn a trade at a distance, than to let him idle about at home; for Jack always preferred bird's-nesting and marbles to any other employment. He would trifle away half the day, when his father thought he was at school, with any boys he could meet who were as idle as himself; and never could be prevailed upon to do or to learn any thing while a game at taw[1] could be had, for love or money. All this time his little brothers,

1 Taw—a game of marbles.

much younger than himself, were beginning to follow the plough, or to carry the corn to mill as soon as they were able to mount a cart-horse.

Jack, however, who was a lively boy, and did not naturally want either sense or good nature, might have turned out well enough, if he had not had the misfortune to be his mother's favorite. She concealed and forgave all his faults. To be sure, he was a little wild, she would say, but he would not make the worse man for that, for Jack had a good spirit of his own, and she would not have it broke, and so make a mope of the boy.

The farmer, for a quiet life as it is called, gave up all these points to his wife; and with them, gave up the future virtue and happiness of his child. He was a laborious and industrious man, but he had no religion: he thought only of the gains and advantages of the present day, and never took the future into the account. His wife managed him entirely, and as she was really notable, he did not trouble his head about any thing farther. If she had been careless in her dairy, he would have stormed and sworn; but as she only ruined one child by indulgence, and almost broke the hearts of the rest by unkindness, he gave himself little concern about the matter.

The cheese certainly was good, and that indeed is a great point; but she was neglectful of her children, and a tyrant to her servants. Her husband's substance, indeed, was not wasted, but his happiness was not consulted. His house, it is true, was not dirty, but it was the abode of fury, ill-temper, and covetousness. And the farmer, though he did not care for drink, was too often driven to the public-house[1] in an evening, because his own was neither quiet nor comfortable. The mother was always scolding, and the children were always crying.

Jack, however, notwithstanding his idleness, picked up a little reading and writing, but never would learn to cast an account; that was too much labor. His mother was desirous he should continue at school, not so much for the sake of his learning, which she had not sense enough to value, but to save her darling from the fatigue of labor; for if he had not gone to school, she knew he must have gone to work, and she thought the former was the least tiresome of the two. Indeed, this foolish woman had such an opinion of his genius, that she used, from a child, to think he was too wise for any thing but a parson, and hoped she should live to see him one. She did not wish to see her son a minister because she loved either learning or piety, but because she thought it would make Jack a gentleman, and set him above his brothers.

Farmer Brown still hoped, that though Jack was likely to make but an idle and ignorant farmer, yet he might make no bad tradesman, when he should be removed from the indulgences of a father's house, and from a silly mother

1 Public-house—pub or drinking establishment.

whose fondness kept him back in every thing. This woman was enraged when she found that so fine a scholar as she took Jack to be, was to be put apprentice to a shoemaker. The farmer, however, for the first time in his life, would have his own way. But being a worldly man, and too apt to mind only what is falsely called *the main chance*, instead of being careful to look out for a sober, prudent, and religious master for his son, he left all that to accident, as if it had been a thing of little or no consequence.

This is a very common fault; and fathers who are guilty of it, are in a great measure answerable for the future sins and errors of their children, when they come out into the world, and set up for themselves. If a man gives his son a good education, a good example, and a good master, it is indeed *possible* that the son may not turn out well, but it does not often happen: and when it does, the father has no blame resting on him; and it is a great point towards a man's comfort to have his conscience quiet in that respect, however God may think fit to overrule events.

The farmer, however, took care to desire his friends to inquire for a shoemaker who had good business, and was a good workman; and the mother did not forget to put in her word, and "desired that it might be one who was not *too strict*; for Jack had been brought up tenderly, was a meek boy, and could not bear to be contradicted in any thing." And this is the common notion of meekness among people who do not take up their notions on rational and Christian grounds.

Mr. Williams was recommended to the farmer as being the best shoemaker in the town in which he lived, and far from a strict master: so, without farther inquiries, to Mr. Williams he went.

James Stock, who was the son of an honest laborer in the next village, was bound out by the parish, in consideration of his father having so numerous a family that he was not able to put him out himself. James was in every thing the very reverse of his new companion. He was a modest, industrious, pious youth; and though so poor, and the child of a laborer, was a much better scholar than Jack, who was a wealthy farmer's son. His father had, it is true, been able to give him but very little schooling, for he was obliged to be put to work when quite a child.

When very young he used to run of errands for Mr. Thomas, the curate of the parish, a very kind-hearted young gentleman, who boarded next door to his father's cottage. He used also to rub down and saddle his horse, and do any other little job for him, in the most civil, obliging manner. All this so recommended him to the clergyman, that he would often send for him in an evening after he had done his day's work in the field, and condescended to teach him himself to write and cast accounts, as well as to instruct him in the principles of religion. It was not merely out of kindness for the little good-natured services James did him, that he showed him this favor, but also for his readiness in the catechism and his devout behavior at church.

The first thing that drew the minister's attention to this boy was the following. He had frequently given him half-pence and pence for holding his horse and carrying him to water, before he was big enough to be further useful to him. On Christmas Day he was surprised to see James at church, reading out of a handsome new prayer-book: he wondered how he came by it, for he knew there was nobody in the parish likely to have given it to him, for at that time there were no Sunday-schools; and the father could not afford it, he was sure.

"Well, James," said he, as he saw him when they came out, "you made a good figure at church today; it made you look like a man and a Christian, to have so handsome a book, and to be so ready in using it. How came you by that book?" James owned modestly, that he had been a whole year saving up the money by single half-pence, all of which had been of the minister's own giving; and that in all that time he had not spent a single farthing on his own diversions.

"My dear boy," said good Mr. Thomas, "I am much mistaken if thou dost not turn out well in the world, for two reasons: first, from thy saving turn and self-denying temper; and next, because thou didst devote the first eighteen pence thou wast ever worth in the world to so good a purpose."

James bowed and blushed, and from that time Mr. Thomas began to take more notice of him, and to instruct him as I said above. As James soon grew able to do him more considerable service, he would now and then give him sixpence. This he constantly saved, till it became a little sum, with which he bought shoes and stockings; well knowing that his poor father, with a large family and low wages, could not buy them for him. As to what little money he earned himself by his daily labor in the field, he constantly carried it to his mother every Saturday night, to buy bread for the family, which was a pretty help to them.

As James was not over stout in his make, his father thankfully accepted the offer of the parish officers to bind out his son to a trade. This good man, however, had not, like farmer Brown, the liberty of choosing a master for his son, or he would carefully have inquired if he was a proper man to have the care of youth; but Williams the shoemaker was already fixed on by those who were to put the boy out, who told him if he wanted a master it must be him or none; for the overseers had a better opinion of Williams than he deserved, and thought it would be the making of the boy to go to him. The father knew that beggars must not be choosers, so he fitted out James for his new place, having indeed little to give him besides his blessing.

The worthy Mr. Thomas, however, kindly gave him an old coat and waistcoat, which his mother, who was a neat and notable woman, contrived to make up for him herself without a farthing expense, and when it was turned and made fit for his size, it made him a very handsome suit for Sundays, and lasted him a couple of years.

And here let me stop to remark, what a pity it is that poor women so seldom are able or willing to do this sort of little handy jobs themselves; and that they do not oftener bring up their daughters to be more useful in family work. They are great losers by it every way; not only as they are disqualifying their girls from making good wives hereafter, but they are losers in point of present advantage; for the wealthy could much oftener afford to give a poor boy a jacket or a waistcoat, if it was not for the expense of making it, which adds very much to the cost.

To my certain knowledge, many poor women would often get an old coat, or a bit of coarse new cloth given them to fit out a boy, if the mothers or sisters were known to be able to cut it out to advantage, and to make it up decently themselves. But half a crown for the making a bit of kersey,[1] which costs but a few shillings, is more than many very charitable people can afford to give—so they often give nothing at all, when they see the mothers so little able to turn it to advantage. It is hoped they will take this hint kindly, as it is meant for their good.

But to return to our two young shoemakers. They were both now settled at Mr. Williams', who,

1 Kersey—a type of coarse fabric.

as he was known to be a good workman, had plenty of business. He had sometimes two or three journeymen, but no apprentices but Jack and James.

Jack, who, with all his faults, was a keen, smart boy, took to learn the trade quick enough; but the difficulty was to make him stick two hours together to his work. At every noise he heard in the street, down went the work—the last[1] one way, the upper leather another; the sole dropped on the ground, and the thread he dragged after him all the way up the street. If a blind fiddler, a ballad-singer, a mountebank, a dancing bear, or a drum, were heard at a distance, out ran Jack; nothing could stop him, and not a stitch more could he be prevailed on to do that day. Every duty, every promise was forgot for the present pleasure; he could not resist the smallest temptation; he never stopped for a moment to consider whether a thing was right or wrong, but whether he liked it or disliked it. And as his ill-judging mother took care to send him privately a good supply of pocket-money, that deadly bane to all youthful virtue, he had generally a few pence ready to spend, and to indulge in the present diversion whatever it was.

And what was still worse even than spending his money, he spent his time too, or rather his master's time. Of this he was continually reminded by James, to whom he always answered, "What have you to complain about? It is nothing

1 Last—a foot shaped form used by shoemakers.

EVERY NOISE HE HEARD ON THE STREET,
DOWN WENT HIS WORK.

to you, or any one else; I spend nobody's money but my own."

"That may be," replied the other, "but you cannot say it is your own time that you spend."

He insisted upon it that it was; but James fetched down their indentures, and there showed him that he had solemnly bound himself, by that instrument, not to waste his master's property.

"Now," quoth James, "thy own time is a very valuable part of thy master's property."

To this he replied, "Every one's time is his own, and he should not sit moping all day over his last; for his part, he thanked God *he* was no *parish 'prentice.*"

James did not resent this piece of foolish impertinence, as some silly lads would have done, nor fly into a violent passion; for even at this early age he had begun to learn of Him "who was meek and lowly of heart;"[1] and therefore, "when he was reviled, he reviled not again." On the contrary, he was so very kind and gentle, that even Jack, vain and idle as he was, could not help loving him, though he took care never to follow his advice.

Jack's fondness for his boyish and silly diversions in the street, soon produced the effects which might naturally be expected; and the same idleness which led him to fly out into the town at the sound of a fiddle, or the sight

1 Matthew 11:29—Take my yoke upon you, and learn of me; for I am meek and lowly in heart: and ye shall find rest unto your souls.

of a puppet-show, soon led him to those places where all these fiddles and shows naturally lead—I mean the ALE-HOUSE. The acquaintance picked up in the street was carried on at the Greyhound; and the idle pastimes of the boy soon led to the destructive vices of the man.

As he was not an ill-tempered youth, nor naturally much given to drink, a sober and prudent master, who had been steady in his management and regular in his own conduct, who would have recommended good advice by a good example, might have made something of Jack. But I am sorry to say, that Mr. Williams, though a good workman and not a very hard or severe master, was neither a sober nor a steady man: so far from it, that he spent much more time at the Greyhound than at home. There was no order either in his shop or family. He left the chief care of the business to his two young apprentices; and being but a worldly man, he was at first disposed to show favor to Jack much more than to James, because he had more money, and his father was better in the world than the father of poor James.

At first, therefore, he was disposed to consider James as a sort of drudge, who was to do all the menial work of the family, and he did not care how little he taught him of his trade. With Mrs. Williams the matter was still worse; she constantly called him away from the business of his trade to wash the house, nurse the child, turn the spit, or run of errands.

And here I must remark, that though parish apprentices are bound in duty to be submissive to both master and mistress, and always to make themselves as useful as they can in a family, and to be civil and humble, yet, on the other hand, it is the duty of masters always to remember, that if they are paid for instructing them in their trade, they ought conscientiously to instruct them in it, and not to employ them the greater part of their time in such household or other drudgery, as to deprive them of the opportunity of acquiring their trade. This practice is not the less unjust because it is common.

Mr. Williams soon found out that his favorite Jack would be of little use to him in the shop; for though he worked well enough, he did not care how little he did. Nor could he be of the least use to his master in keeping an account, or writing out a bill upon occasion; for as he never could be made to learn to cipher, he did not know addition from multiplication.

One day one of the customers called at the shop in a great hurry, and desired his bill might he made out that minute. Mr. Williams, having taken a cup too much, made several attempts to put down a clear account; but the more he tried, the less he found himself able to do it.

James, who was sitting at his last, rose up, and with great modesty asked his master if he would please to give him leave to make out the bill, saying, that though but a poor scholar, he would do his best, rather than keep the gentleman waiting.

Williams gladly accepted his offer; and confused as his head was with liquor, he yet was able to observe with what neatness, dispatch, and exactness, the account was drawn out.

From that time he no longer considered James as a drudge, but as one fitted for the higher employments of the trade; and he was now regularly employed to manage the accounts, with which all the customers were so well pleased that it contributed greatly to raise him in his master's esteem; for there were now never any of those blunders or false charges for which the shop had before been so famous.

James went on in a regular course of industry, and soon became the best workman Mr. Williams had; but there were many things in the family which he greatly disapproved. Some of the journeymen used to swear, drink, and sing very licentious songs. All these things were a great grief to his sober mind: he complained to his master, who only laughed at him; and indeed, as Williams did the same himself, he put it out of his own power to correct his servants, if he had been so disposed. James, however, used always to reprove them, with great mildness indeed, but with great seriousness also. This, but still more his own excellent example, produced at length very good effects on such of the men as were not quite hardened in sin.

What grieved him most was the manner in which the Sabbath was spent. The master lay in bed all the morning; nor did the mother or her children ever go to church, except there was some new finery to be shown, or a christening to be attended. The town's people were coming to the shop all the morning for work which should have been sent home the night before, had not the master been at the alehouse.

And what wounded James to the very soul was, that the master expected the two apprentices to carry home shoes to the country customers on Sunday morning; which he wickedly thought was a saving of time, as it prevented their hindering their work on the Saturday. These shameful practices greatly afflicted poor James; he begged his master, with tears in his eyes, to excuse him, but he only laughed at his squeamish conscience, as he called it.

Jack did not dislike this part of the business, and generally, after he had delivered his parcel, wasted a good part of the day in nutting, playing at fives, or dropping in at the public-house: any thing was better to Jack than going to church.

James, on the other hand, when he was compelled sorely against his conscience to carry home any goods on a Sunday morning, always got up as soon as it was light, knelt down, and prayed heartily to God to forgive him a sin which it was not in his power to avoid; he took care not to lose a moment by the way, but as he was taking his walk with the utmost speed to leave his shoes with the customers, he spent his time in endeavoring to keep up good thoughts in his mind, and praying that the day might come when his conscience might be delivered from this grievous burden. He was now particularly thankful that Mr. Thomas had formerly taught him so many psalms and chapters, which he used to repeat in these walks with great devotion.

He always got home before the rest of the family were up, dressed himself very clean, and went twice to church; and as he greatly disliked the company and practices of his master's house, particularly on the Sabbath-day, he preferred spending his evening alone, reading his Bible, which I forgot to say the worthy clergyman had given him when he left his native village.

Sunday evening, which is to some people such a burden, was to James the highest holiday. He had formerly learned a little how to sing a psalm of the clerk of his own parish, and this was now become a very delightful part of his evening exercise. And as Will Simpson, one of the journeymen, by James' advice and example, was now beginning to be of a more serious way of thinking, he often asked him to sit an hour with him, when they read the Bible and talked it over together in a manner very pleasant and improving; and as Will was a famous singer, a psalm or two sung together was a very innocent pleasure.

James' good manners and civility to the customers drew much business to the shop; and his skill as a workman was so great, that every one desired his shoes might be made by James. Williams grew so very idle and negligent, that he now totally neglected his affairs, and to hard drinking added deep gaming.

All James' care, both of the shop and the accounts, could not keep things in any tolerable order: he represented to his master that they were growing worse and worse; and exhorted him, if he valued his credit as a tradesman, his comfort as a husband and father, his character as a master, and his soul as a Christian, to turn over a new leaf. Williams swore a great oath that he would not be restrained in his pleasures to please a canting parish 'prentice, nor to humor a parcel of squalling brats—that let people say what they would of him, they should never say he was a *hypocrite*; and as long as they could not call him that, he did not care what else they called him.

In a violent passion he immediately went to the Greyhound, where he now spent, not only every evening, which he had long done, but good part of the day and night also. His wife was very dressy, extravagant, and fond of company, and wasted at home as fast as her husband spent abroad; so that all the neighbors said, if it had not been for James, his master must have broke long ago, but they were sure he could not hold out much longer.

As Jack Brown sung a good song, and played many diverting tricks, Williams liked his company, and often allowed him to make one at the Greyhound, where he would laugh heartily at his stories. Every one thought Jack was much the greater favorite, and so he was as a companion in frolic, and foolery, and *pleasure*, as it is called; but Williams would not trust him with an inch of leather, or sixpence in money. No, no; when business was to be done, or trust was to be reposed; James was the man: the idle and the drunken never trust one another, if they have common sense. They like to laugh, and sing, and riot, and drink together; but when they want a friend, a counselor, a helper in business or in trouble, they go farther afield. Williams, while he would drink with Jack, would trust James with untold gold; and even was foolishly tempted to neglect his business the more, from knowing that he had one at home who was taking care of it.

In spite of all James care and diligence, however, things were growing worse and worse: the more James saved, the more his master and mistress spent. One morning, just as the shop was opened, and James had set every body to their respective work, and he himself was settling the business for the day, he found that his master had not yet come from the Greyhound. As this was now become a common case, he only grieved, but did not wonder at it. While he was indulging sad thoughts on what would be the end of all this, in ran the tapster from the Greyhound out of breath, and with a look of terror and dismay, desired James would step over to the public-house with him that moment, for that his master wanted him.

James went immediately, surprised at this unusual message. When he got into the kitchen of the public-house, which he now entered for the first time in his life, though it was just opposite the house in which he lived, he was shocked at the beastly, disgusting appearance of every thing he beheld. There was a table covered with tankards, punch-bowls, broken glasses, pipes, and dirty, greasy packs of cards, and all over wet with liquor; the floor was strewed with broken earthen cups, odd cards, and an E O table shivered to pieces in a quarrel; and behind the table stood a crowd of dirty fellows, with matted locks, hollow eyes, and faces smeared with tobacco. James made his way after the tapster, through this wretched looking crew, to a settle which stood in the chimney corner. Not a word was uttered, but the silent horror seemed to denote something more than a mere common drunken bout.

What was the dismay of James, when he saw his miserable master stretched out on the settle in all the agonies of death! He had fallen into a fit, after drinking hard the best part of the night, and seemed to have but a few minutes to live. In his frightful countenance was displayed the dreadful picture of sin and death; for he struggled at once under the guilt of intoxication, and the pangs of a dying man. He recovered his senses for a few moments, and called out to ask if his faithful servant had come. James went up to him, took him by his cold hand, but was too much moved to speak.

"O! James, James," cried he in a broken voice, "pray for me, comfort me."

James spoke kindly to him, but was too honest to give him false comfort, as is too often done by mistaken friends in these dreadful moments.

"James," said he, "I have been a bad master to you—you would have saved my soul and body, but I would not let you—I have ruined my wife, my children, and my own soul. Take warning, O take warning by my miserable end," said he to his stupefied companions; but none were able to attend to him but James, who bade him lift up his heart to God, and prayed heartily for him himself.

"O!" said the dying man, "it is too late, too late for me—but you have still time," said he to the half drunken terrified crew around him. "Where is Jack?"

Jack Brown came forward, but was too much frightened to speak.

"O wretched boy!" said he, "I fear I shall have the ruin of thy soul as well as my own, to answer for. Stop short! Take warning, now, in the days of thy youth. O James, James, thou dost not pray for me. Death is dreadful to the wicked. O the sting of death to a guilty conscience!"

Here he lifted up his ghastly eyes in speechless horror, grasped hard the hand of James, gave a deep hollow groan, and closed his eyes, never to open them but in an awful eternity.

This was death in all its horrors! The gay companions of his sinful pleasures could not stand the sight; all slunk away, like guilty thieves, from their late favorite friend—no one was left to assist him but his two apprentices. Brown was not so hardened but that he shed many tears for his unhappy master, and even made some hasty resolutions of amendment, which were too soon forgotten.

While Brown stepped home to call the workmen to come and assist in removing their poor master, James stayed alone with the corpse, and employed those awful moments in indulging the most serious thoughts, and praying heartily to God that so terrible a lesson might not be thrown away upon him, but that he might be enabled to live in a constant state of preparation for death. The resolutions he made at this moment, as they were not made in his own strength, but in a humble reliance on God's gracious help, were of use to him as long as he lived; and if ever he was for a moment tempted to say or do a wrong thing, the remembrance of his poor dying master's last agonies, and the dreadful words he uttered, instantly checked him.

When Williams was buried, and his affairs came to be inquired into, they were found to be in a sad condition. His wife, indeed, was the less to be pitied, as she had contributed her full share to the common ruin. James, however, did pity her, and by his skill in accounts, his known honesty, and the trust the creditors put in his word, things came to be settled rather better than Mrs. Williams expected.

Both Brown and James were now within a month or two of being out of their time. The creditors, as was said before, employed James to settle his late master's accounts, which he did in a manner so creditable to his abilities and his honesty, that they proposed to him to take the shop himself. He assured them it was utterly out of his power for want of money. As the creditors had not the least doubt as to their being repaid, if it should please God to spare his life, they generously agreed among themselves to advance him a small sum of money without any security but his bond. For this he was to pay a very reasonable interest, and to return the whole in a given number of years. James shed tears of gratitude at this testimony to his character, and could hardly be prevailed on to accept their kindness, so great was his dread of being in debt.

He took the remainder of the lease from his mistress, and in settling affairs with her, took care to make every thing as advantageous to her as possible. He never once allowed himself to think how unkind she had been to him; he only saw in her the needy widow of his deceased master, and the distressed mother of an infant family, and was heartily sorry it was not in his power to contribute to their support: it was not only his duty, but his delight to return good for evil—for he was a CHRISTIAN.

James Stock was now, by the blessing of God on his own earnest endeavors, master of a considerable shop, and was respected by the whole town for his prudence, honesty, and piety. How he behaved in his station, and also what befell his comrade Brown, must be the subject of another book; and I hope my readers will look forward with some impatience for some further account of this worthy young man. In the meantime, other apprentices will do well to follow so praiseworthy an example, and to remember, that the respectable master of a large shop, and a profitable business, was raised to that creditable situation, without money, friends, or connections, from the low beginning of a *parish apprentice*, by sobriety, industry, *the fear of God*, and an obedience to the divine principles of the CHRISTIAN RELIGION.

PART II

THE APPRENTICE TURNED MASTER

THE first part of this history left off with the dreadful, sudden death of Williams, the idle shoemaker, who died in a drunken fit at the Greyhound. It also showed how James Stock, his faithful apprentice, by his honest and upright behavior, so gained the love and respect of his late master's creditors, that they set him up in business, though he was not worth a shilling of his own, such is the power of a good character. And when we last parted from him he had just got possession of his master's shop.

This sudden prosperity was a time of trial for James; who, as he had now become a creditable tradesman, I shall hereafter think proper to call Mr. James Stock. I say, this sudden rise in life was a time of trial; for we hardly know what we are ourselves till we become our own masters. There is, indeed, always a reasonable hope that a good servant will not make a bad master, and that a faithful apprentice will prove an honest tradesman. But the heart of man is deceitful, and some folks who seem to behave very well while they are under subjection, no sooner get a little power than their heads are turned, and they grow prouder than those who are gentlemen born. They forget at once that they were lately poor and dependent themselves, so that one would think that with their poverty they had lost their memory too. I have known some who had suffered most hardships in their early days, become the most hard and oppressive in their turn; so that they seem to forget that fine considerate reason which God gives to the children of Israel why they should be merciful to their servants, "remembering," saith he, "that thou thyself wast a bondman."[1]

Young Mr. Stock did not so forget himself. He had indeed the only sure guard from falling into this error. It was not from any easiness in his natural disposition; for that only just serves to make folks good-natured when they are pleased, and patient when they have nothing to vex them. James went upon higher ground. He brought his religion into all his actions; he did not give way to abusive language, because he knew it was a sin. He did not use his apprentices ill, because he knew he had himself a Master in heaven.

He knew he owed his present happy situation to the kindness of the creditors. But did he grow easy and careless because he knew he

1 Deuteronomy 15:15—And thou shalt remember that thou wast a bondman in the land of Egypt, and the LORD thy God redeemed thee: therefore I command thee this thing to day.

had such friends? No, indeed. He worked with double diligence in order to get out of debt, and to let these friends see he did not abuse their kindness. Such behavior as this is the greatest encouragement in the world to rich people to lend a little money. It creates friends, and it keeps them.

His shoes and boots were made in the best manner—this *got* him business; he set out with a rule to tell no lies and deceive no customers—this *secured* his business. He had two reasons for not promising to send home goods when he knew he should not be able to keep his word. The first, because he knew a lie was a sin; the next, because it was a folly. There is no credit sooner worn out than that which is gained by false pretences. After a little while no one is deceived by them. Falsehood is so soon found out, that I believe most tradesmen are the poorer for it in the long run. Deceit is the worst part of a shopkeeper's stock in trade.

James was now at the head of a family. "This is a serious situation," said he to himself, one fine summer's evening, as he stood leaning over the half-door of his shop, to enjoy a little fresh air. "I am now master of a family. My cares are doubled, and so are my duties. I see the higher one gets in life, the more one has to answer for. Let me now call to mind the sorrow I used to feel when I was made to carry work home on a Sunday by an ungodly master; and let me now *keep* the resolutions I then formed."

So, what his heart found right to do, he resolved to do quickly; and he set out at first as he meant to go on. The Sabbath was truly a day of rest at Mr. Stock's. He would not allow a pair of shoes to be given out on that day to oblige the best customer he had. And what did he lose by it? Why, nothing. For, when the people were once used to it, they liked Saturday night just as well. But had it been otherwise, he would have given up his gains to his conscience.

Showing How Mr. Stock Behaved to His Apprentices.

When he got up in the world so far as to have apprentices, he thought himself as accountable for their behavior as if they had been his children. He was very kind to them, and had a cheerful, merry way of talking to them; so that the lads, who had seen too much of swearing, reprobate masters, were very fond of him. They were never afraid of speaking to him; they told him all their little troubles, and considered their master as their best friend, for they said they would do any thing for a good word and a kind look. As he did not swear at them when they had been guilty of a fault, they did not lie to him to conceal it, and thereby make one fault two.

But though he was very kind, he was very watchful also, for he did not think neglect any part of kindness. He brought them to adopt one very pretty method, which was, on a Sunday evening, to divert themselves with writing out half a dozen texts of scripture in a pretty copybook with gilt covers. You may have the same at any of the stationers; they do not cost above fourpence, and will last nearly a year.

When the boys carried him their books, he justly commended him whose texts were written in the fairest hand. "And now, my boys," said he, "let us see which of you will learn your texts best in the course of the week; he who does this shall choose for next Sunday."

Thus the boys soon got many psalms and chapters by heart, almost without knowing how they came by them. He taught them how to make a practical use of what they learned; "for," said he, "it will answer little purpose to learn texts, if we do not try to live up to them."

One of the boys being apt to play in his absence, and to run back again to his work when he heard his master's step, he brought him to a sense of his fault by the last Sunday's text, which happened to be the sixth of Ephesians. He showed him what was meant by being "obedient to his master in singleness of heart, as unto Christ," and explained to him with so much kindness what it was, not to work "with eye-service, as men-pleasers, but doing the will of God from the heart," that the lad said he should never forget it, and it did more towards curing him of idleness than the soundest horsewhipping would have done.

How Mr. Stock Got out of Debt.

Stock's behavior was very regular, and he was much beloved for his kind and peaceable temper.

He also had a good reputation for skill in his trade, and his industry was talked of through the whole town, so that he had soon more work than he could possibly do. He paid all his dealers to the very day, and took care to carry his interest money to the creditors the moment it became due. In two or three years he was able to begin to pay off a small part of the principal.

His reason for being so eager to pay money as soon as it became due was this: he had observed tradesmen, and especially his old master, put off the day of payment as long as they could, even though they had the means in their power. This deceived them; for having money in their pockets, they forgot it belonged to the creditor, and not to themselves, and so got to fancy they were rich, when they were really poor. This false notion led them to indulge in idle expenses; whereas, if they had paid regularly, they would have had this one temptation the less. A young tradesman, when he is going to spend money, should at least ask himself whether this money is his own or his creditors'. This little question might help to prevent many a bankruptcy.

A true Christian always goes heartily to work to find out what is his besetting sin; and when he has found it—which he easily may, if he looks sharp—against this sin he watches narrowly. I know it is the fashion among some folks—and a bad fashion it is—to fancy that good people have no sin; but this only shows their ignorance. It is not true. That good man St. Paul knew better. See Romans 7. And when men do not own their sins, it is not because there is no sin in their hearts, but because they are not anxious to search for it, nor humble to confess it, nor penitent to mourn over it. But this was not the case with James Stock. "Examine yourselves truly," said he, "is no bad part of the catechism."

He began to be afraid that his desire of living creditably, and without being a burden to any one, might, under the mask of honesty and independence, lead him into pride and covetousness. He feared that the bias of his heart lay that way. So, instead of being proud of his sobriety; instead of bragging that he never spent his money idly, nor went to the alehouse; instead of boasting how hard he worked, and how he denied himself, he strove in secret that even these good qualities might not grow out of a wrong root. The following event was of use to him in the way of indulging any disposition to covetousness.

One evening, as he was standing at the door of his shop, a poor dirty boy, without stockings and shoes, came up and asked him for a bit of broken victuals, for he had eaten nothing all day. In spite of his dirt and rags he was a very pretty, lively, civil-spoken boy, and Mr. Stock could not help thinking he knew something of his face. He fetched him out a good piece of bread and cheese, and while the boy was devouring it, asked him if he had no parents, and why he went about in that vagabond manner.

"Daddy has been dead for some years," said the boy; "he died in a fit over at the Greyhound. Mammy says he used to live at this shop, and then we did not want for clothes nor victuals neither."

Stock was melted almost to tears on finding that this dirty beggar-boy was Tommy Williams, the son of his old master. He blessed God on comparing his own happy condition with that of this poor destitute child, but he was not proud at the comparison; and while he was thankful for his own prosperity, he pitied the helpless boy.

"Where have you been living of late?" said he to him, "for I understood you all went home to your mother's friends."

"So we did, sir," said the boy, "but they are grown tired of maintaining us, because they said that mammy spent all the money which should have gone to buy victuals for us, on snuff and drams. And so they have sent us back to this place, which is daddy's parish."

"And where do you live here?" said Mr. Stock.

"O, sir, we are all put into the parish poorhouse."

"And does your mother do any thing to help to maintain you?"

"No, sir, for mammy says she was not brought up to work like poor folks, and she would rather starve than spin or knit; so she lies abed all the morning, and sends us about to pick up what we can, a bit of victuals or a few halfpence."

MR. STOCK FETCHED HIM A GOOD PIECE
OF BREAD AND CHEESE.

"And have you any money in your pocket now?"

"Yes, sir, I have got three halfpence which I have begged today."

"Then, as you were so very hungry, how came you not to buy a roll at that baker's over the way?"

"Because, sir, I was going to lay it out in tea for mammy, for I never lay out a farthing for myself. Indeed, mammy says she *will* have her tea twice a day, if we beg or starve for it."

"Can you read, my boy?" said Mr. Stock.

"A little, sir, and say my prayers, too."

"And can you say your catechism?"

"I have almost forgot it all, sir, though I remember something about 'honoring my father and mother,' and that makes me still carry the halfpence home to mammy, instead of buying cakes."

"Who taught you these good things?"

"One Jemmy Stock, sir, who was a parish 'prentice to my daddy. He taught me one question out of the catechism every night, and always made me say my prayers to him before I went to bed. He told me I should go to the wicked place if I did not fear God; so I am still afraid to tell lies like the other boys. Poor Jemmy gave me a piece of gingerbread every time I learned well; but I have no friend now: Jemmy was very good to me, though mammy did nothing but beat him."

Mr. Stock was too much moved to carry on the discourse; he did not make himself known to the boy, but took him over to the baker's shop. As they walked along, he could not help repeating aloud a verse or two of that beautiful hymn, so deservedly the favorite of all children:

"Not more than others I deserve,
Yet God hath given me more;
For I have food while others starve,
Or beg from door to door,"[1]

The little boy looked up in his face, saying, "Why, sir, that's the very hymn which Jemmy Stock gave me a penny for learning." Stock made no answer, but put a couple of three-penny loaves into his hand to carry home, and told him to call on him again at such a time in the following week.

How Mr. Stock Contrived to Be Charitable without Any Expense.

Stock had abundant subject for meditation that night. He was puzzled what to do with the boy. While he was carrying on his trade upon borrowed money, he did not think it right to give any part of that money to assist the idle, or even to help the distressed. "I must be just," said he, "before I am generous." Still, he could not bear to see this fine boy given up to certain ruin. He did not think it safe to take him into his shop, in his present ignorant, unprincipled state. At last he hit upon this thought: "I work for myself twelve hours in the day. Why shall I not work

1 Isaac Watts, "Praise For Daily Mercies."

one hour or two for this boy in the evening? It will be but for a year, and I shall then have more right to do what I please. My money will then be my own, I shall have paid my debts."

So he began to put his resolution in practice that very night, sticking to his old notion of not putting off till tomorrow what should be done today; and it was thought he owed much of his success in life, as well as his growth in goodness, to this little saying. "I am young and healthy," said he; "one hour's work more will do me no harm: I will set aside all I get by these over-hours, and put the boy to school. I have not only no right to punish this child for the sins of his father, but I consider that though God hateth those sins, he has made them instruments for my advancement."

Tommy Williams called at the time appointed. In the meantime, Mr. Stock's maid had made him a tidy little suit of clothes out of an old coat of her master's. She had also knit him a pair of stockings, and Mr. Stock made him sit down in the shop while he himself fitted him with a pair of new shoes.

The maid having washed and dressed him, Mr. Stock took him by the hand, and walked along with him to the parish poor-house to find his mother. They found her dressed in ragged, filthy finery, standing at the door, where she passed most of her time quarrelling with half a dozen women as idle and dirty as herself: when she saw Tommy so neat and well-dressed, she fell a crying for joy. She said it put her in mind of old times, for Tommy always used to be dressed like a gentleman.

"So much the worse," said Mr. Stock; "if you had not begun by making him look like a gentleman, you needed not have ended by making him look like a beggar."

"O, Jem!" said she—for though it was four years since she had seen him, she soon recollected him—"fine times for you; 'set a beggar on horseback'—you know the proverb. I shall beat Tommy well for finding you out, and exposing me to you."

Instead of entering into any dispute with this bad woman, or praising himself at her expense; instead of putting her in mind of her past ill behavior to him, or reproaching her with the bad use she had made of her prosperity, he mildly said to her, "Mrs. Williams, I am sorry for your misfortunes: I am come to relieve you of part of your burden; I will take Tommy off your hands. I will give him a year's board and schooling, and by that time I shall see what he is fit for. I will promise nothing, but if the boy turns out well, I will never forsake him. I shall make but one bargain with you, which is, that he must not come to this place to hear all this railing and swearing, nor shall he keep company with these pilfering, idle children. You are welcome to go and see him when you please, but here he must not come."

The foolish woman burst out a-crying, saying, she should lose her poor dear Tommy forever.

Mr. Stock might give *her* the money he intended to pay at the school, for nobody could do so well by him as his own mother.

The truth was, she wanted to get these new clothes into her clutches, which would all have been pawned at the dram-shop before the week was out. This Mr. Stock well knew. From crying she fell to scolding and swearing. She told him he was an unnatural wretch, that wanted to make a child despise his own mother because she was poor. She even went so far as to say she would not part from him; she said she hated your godly people; they had no bowels of compassion, but tried to set men, women, and children against their own flesh and blood.

Mr. Stock now almost lost his patience, and for one moment a thought came across him to strip the boy, carry back the clothes, and leave him to his unnatural mother. "Why," said he, "should I work over-hours, and wear out my strength for this wicked woman?" But he soon checked this thought, by reflecting on the patience and long-suffering of God with rebellious sinners. This cured his anger in a moment, and he mildly reasoned with her on her folly and blindness in opposing the good of her child.

One of the neighbors who stood by, said, "what a fine thing it was for the boy, but some people were born to be lucky. She wished Mr. Stock would take a fancy to *her* child, he should have him soon enough."

Mrs. Williams now began to be frightened

lest Mr. Stock should take the woman at her word, and sullenly consented to let the boy go, from envy and malice, not from prudence and gratitude; and Tommy was sent to school that very night, his mother crying and roaring, instead of thanking God for such a blessing.

And here I cannot forbear telling a very good-natured thing of Will Simpson, one of the workmen. By-the-by, it was that very young fellow who was reformed by Stock's good example, when he was an apprentice, and who used to sing psalms with him on a Sunday evening, when they got out of the way of Williams' junketing. Will coming home early one evening, was surprised to find his master at work by himself, long after the usual time. He begged so heartily to know the reason, that Stock owned the truth. Will was so struck with this piece of kindness that he snatched up a last, crying out; "Well, master, you shall not work by yourself, any how; we will go snacks in maintaining Tommy: it shall never be said, that Will Simpson was idling about, when his master was working for charity." This made the hour pass cheerfully, and doubled the profits.

In a year or two, Mr. Stock, by God's blessing on his labors, became quite clear of the world. He now paid of his creditors; but he never forgot his obligation to them, and found many opportunities of showing kindness to them, and to their children after them. He now cast about for a proper wife, and as he was thought a prosperous man, and very well-looking besides, most of the smart girls of the place, with their tawdry finery, used to be often parading before the shop, and would even go to church in order to put themselves in his way. But Mr. Stock when he went to church had other things in his head, and if ever he thought about these gay damsels at all, it was with concern at seeing them so improperly tricked out; so that the very means they took to please him, made him dislike them.

There was one Betsy West, a young woman of excellent character, and very modest appearance. He had seldom seen her out, as she was employed night and day in waiting on an aged widowed mother, who was both lame and blind. This good girl was indeed almost literally eyes and feet to her helpless parent; and Mr. Stock used to see her, through the little casement window, lifting her up, and feeding her with a tenderness which greatly raised his esteem for her. He used to tell Will Simpson, as they sat at work, that such a dutiful daughter could hardly fail to make a faithful wife. He had not, however, the heart to try to draw her off from the care of her sick mother. The poor woman declined very fast. Betsy was much employed in reading or praying by her when she was awake, and passed good part of the night while she slept in doing some fine works to sell, in order to supply her sick mother with the little niceties which their poor pittance could not afford, while she herself lived on a crust.

Mr. Stock knew that Betsy would have little or nothing after her mother's death, as she had only a life income. On the other hand, Mr. Thompson the tanner had offered him two hundred pounds with his daughter Nancy; but he was almost sorry that he had not in this case an opportunity of resisting his natural bias, which rather lay on the side of loving money: "for," said he, "putting principle and putting affection out of the question, I shall do a more *prudent* thing by marrying Betsy West, who will conform to her station, and is a religious, humble, industrious girl, without a shilling, than by having an idle, dressy lass, who will neglect my family, and fill my house with company, though she should have twice the fortune which Nancy Thompson would bring."

At length poor old Mrs. West was released from all her sufferings. At a proper time Mr. Stock proposed marriage to Betsy, and was accepted. All the disappointed girls in the town wondered what any body could like in such a dowdy as that. Had the man no eyes? They thought Mr. Stock had had more taste. O! how it did provoke all the vain, idle things to find, that staying at home, dressing plainly, serving God, and nursing a blind mother, should do that for Betsy West, which all their contrivances, flaunting, and dancing, could not do for them.

He was not disappointed in his hope of meeting with a good wife in Betsy, as indeed those who marry on right grounds seldom are. But if religious persons will, for the sake of money, choose partners for life who have no religion, do not let them complain that they are unhappy; they might have known that beforehand.

Tommy Williams was now taken home to Stock's house and bound apprentice. He was always kind and attentive to his mother; and every penny which Will Simpson or his master gave him for learning a chapter, he would save to buy a bit of tea and sugar for her. When the other boys laughed at him for being so foolish as to deny himself cakes and apples, to give his money to her who was so bad a woman, he would answer, "It may be so, but she is my mother for all that."

Mr. Stock was much moved at the change in this boy, who turned out a very good youth. He resolved, as God should prosper him, that he would try to snatch other helpless creatures from sin and ruin. "For," said he, "it is owing to God's blessing on the instructions of my good minister when I was a child, that I have been saved from the broad way of destruction." He still gave God the glory of every thing he did aright; and when Will Simpson one day said to him, "Master, I wish I were half as good as you are:" "Hold, William," answered he, gravely, "I once read in a book, that the devil is willing enough we should appear to do good actions, if he can but make us proud of them."

But we must not forget our other old acquaintance, Mr. Stock's fellow-'prentice. So, in the next part you may expect a full account of the many tricks and frolics of idle Jack Brown.

PART III

SOME ACCOUNT OF THE FROLICS OF IDLE JACK BROWN

YOU shall now hear what befell idle Jack Brown, who, being a farmer's son, had many advantages to begin life with. But he who wants prudence may be said to want every thing, because he turns all his advantages to no account.

Jack Brown was just out of his time when his master, Williams, died in that terrible drunken fit at the Greyhound. You know already how Stock succeeded to his master's business, and prospered in it. Jack wished very much to enter into partnership with him. His father and mother too were desirous of it, and offered to advance a hundred pounds with him. Here is a fresh proof of the power of a good character! The old farmer, with all his covetousness, was eager to get his son into partnership with Stock, though the latter was not worth a shilling; and even Jack's mother, with all her pride, was eager for it, for they both had sense enough to see it would be the making of Jack. The father knew that Stock would look to the main chance; and the mother that he would take the laboring oar, and so her darling would have little to do. The ruling passion operated in both. One parent wished to secure to the son a life of pleasure; the other a profitable trade. Both were equally indifferent to whatever related to his eternal good.

Stock, however, young as he was, was too old a bird to be caught with chaff. His wisdom was an overmatch for their cunning. He had a kindness for Brown, but would on no account enter into business with him. "One of these three things," said he, "I am sure will happen, if I do: he will either hurt my principles, my character, or my trade; perhaps all."

And here, by-the-by, let me drop a hint to other young men who are about to enter into partnership. Let them not do that in haste which they may repent at leisure. Next to marriage, it is a tie the hardest to break; and next to that, it is an engagement which ought to be entered into with the greatest caution. Many things go to the making such a connection suitable, safe, and pleasant. There is many a rich merchant need not be above taking a hint in this respect from James Stock the shoemaker.

Brown was still unwilling to part from him; indeed, he was too idle to look out for business, so he offered Stock to work with him as a journeyman; but this he also mildly refused. It hurt his good-nature to do so; but he reflected that a young man who has his way to make in the world, must not only be good-natured, he must be prudent also. "I am resolved," said he, "to employ none but the most sober, regular young men I can get. 'Evil communications corrupt good manners;' and I should be answerable for all the disorders of my own house, if I knowingly took a wild, drinking young fellow into it. That which might be kindness to one, would be injustice to many, and therefore a sin in myself."

Brown's mother was in a great rage when she heard that her son had stooped so low as to make this offer. She valued herself on being proud, for she thought pride was a grand thing. Poor woman! She did not know that it is the meanest thing in the world. It was her ignorance which made her proud, as is apt to be the case. "You mean-spirited rascal," said she to Jack, "I had rather follow you to your grave, as well as I love you, than to see you disgrace your family by working under Jem Stock, the parish apprentice." She forgot already what pains she had taken about the partnership, but pride and passion have bad memories.

It is hard to say which now was uppermost in her mind, her desire to be revenged on Stock, or to see her son make a figure. She raised every shilling she could get from her husband, and all she could crib from the dairy, to set up Jack in a showy way. So the very next market-day she came herself, and took for him the new white house, with the two little sash windows painted blue, and blue posts before the door. It is that house which has the old cross just before it, as you turn down between the church and the Greyhound. Its being so near the church to be sure was no recommendation to Jack, but its being so near the Greyhound was; and so taking one thing with the other, it was to be sure no bad situation; but what weighed most with the mother was, that it was a much more showy shop than Stock's; and the house, though not half so convenient, was far more smart.

In order to draw custom, his foolish mother advised him to undersell his neighbors just at first; to buy ordinary but showy goods, and employ cheap workmen. In short, she charged him to leave no stone unturned to ruin his old comrade Stock. Indeed, she always thought with double satisfaction of Jack's prosperity, because she always joined to it the hope that his success would be the ruin of Stock; for she owned it would be the joy of her heart to bring that proud upstart to a morsel of bread. She did not understand, for her part, why such beggars must become tradesmen; it was making a velvet purse of a sow's ear.

Stock, however, set out on quite another set of principles. He did not allow himself always to square his own behavior to others by theirs to him. He seldom asked himself what he should *like* to do; but he had a mighty way of saying, "I wonder, now, what it is my *duty* to do?" And when he was once clear in that matter, he generally did it, always begging God's blessing and direction. So, instead of setting Brown at defiance;

instead of all that vulgar selfishness, of "catch he that catch can," and "two of a trade can never agree," he resolved to be friendly towards him. Instead of joining in the laugh against Brown for making his house so fine, he was sorry for him, because he feared he would never be able to pay such a rent. So he very kindly called upon him, and told him there was business enough for them both, and gave him many useful hints for his going on. He warned him to go oftener to church and seldomer to the Greyhound; put him in mind how following the one and forsaking the other had been the ruin of their poor master, and added the following:

ADVICE TO YOUNG TRADESMEN.

"Buy the best goods; cut the work out yourself; let the eye of the master be everywhere; employ the soberest men; avoid all the low deceits of trade; never lower the credit of another to raise your own; make short payments; keep exact accounts; avoid idle company; and be very strict to your word."

For a short time things went on swimmingly. Brown was merry and civil. The shop was well situated for gossip; and every one who had something to say, and nothing to do, was welcome. Every idle story was first spread, and every idle song first sung in Brown's shop. Every customer who came to be measured was promised that his shoes should be done first. But the misfortune was, if twenty came in a day, the same promise was made to all; so that nineteen were disappointed, and of course affronted. He never said "No" to any one. It is indeed a word which it requires some honesty to pronounce. By all these false promises he was thought the most obliging fellow that ever made a shoe. And as he set out on the principle of underselling, people took a mighty fancy to the cheap shop. And it was agreed among all the young and giddy, that he would beat Stock hollow, and that the old shop would soon be knocked up.

All Is Not Gold That Glistens.

After a few months, however, folks began to be not quite so fond of the cheap shop; one found out that the leather was bad, another that the work was slight. Those who liked substantial goods went all of them to Stock's, for they said Brown's heel-taps did not last a week; his new boots let in water; and they believed he made his soles of brown paper. Besides, it was thought by most, that his promising to all, and keeping his word with none, hurt his business as much as any thing. Indeed, I question, putting religion out of the case, if lying ever answers even in a political view.

Brown had what is commonly called a *good heart*; that is, he had a thoughtless good-nature, and a sort of feeling for the moment which made him seem sorry when others were in trouble.

But he was not apt to put himself to any inconvenience, nor go a step out of his way, nor give up any pleasure to serve the best friend he had. He loved fun; and those who do, should always see that it be harmless, and that they do not give up more for it than it is worth. I am not going to say a word against innocent merriment. I like it myself, but what the proverb says of gold, may be said of mirth: it may be bought too dear. If a young man finds that what he fancies is a good joke may possibly offend God, hurt his neighbor, afflict his parent, or make a modest girl blush, let him then be assured it is not fun but wickedness, and he had better let it alone.

Jack Brown, then, as *good a heart* as he had, did not know what it was to deny himself any thing. He was so *good-natured*, indeed, that he never in his life refused to make one of a jolly set; but he was not good-natured enough to consider, that those men whom he kept up all night roaring and laughing, had wives and children at home, who had little to eat, and less to wear, because *they* were keeping up the character of merry fellows and good hearts at the public-house.

The Mountebank.[1]

One day he saw his father's ploughboy come galloping up to his door in great haste. This boy brought Brown word that his mother was dangerously ill, and that his father had sent his own best bay mare, Smiler, that his son might lose

1 Mountebank—a performer who sells quack medicines.

no time, but set out directly to see his mother before she died. Jack burst into tears, lamented the danger of so fond a mother, and all the people in the shop extolled his *good heart*.

He sent back the boy directly, with a message that he would follow him in half an hour, as soon as the mare had baited; for he well knew that his father would not thank him for any haste he might make, if Smiler was hurt.

Jack accordingly set off, and rode with such speed to the next town, that both himself and Smiler had a mind to another bait. They stopped at the Star; unluckily it was fair-day, and as he was walking about while Smiler was eating her oats, a bill was put into his hand, setting forth, that on a stage opposite the Globe, a mountebank was showing away, and his Andrew[1] performing the finest tricks that ever were seen. He read—he stood still—he went on: "It will not hinder me," says he; "Smiler must rest; and I shall see my poor dear mother quite as soon if I just take a peep, as if I sit moping at the Star."

The tricks were so merry that the time seemed short; and when they were over, he could not forbear going into the Globe and treating these choice spirits with a bowl of punch. Just as they were taking the last glass, Jack happened to say that he was the best fives-player[2] in the country.

"That is lucky," said the Andrew; "for there

1 Andrew—also "Merry Andrew," the mountebank's assistant.

2 Fives—a game with a ball played against a wall.

is a famous match now playing in the court, and you may never again have such an opportunity to show your skill."

Brown declared he could not stay, for that he had left his horse at the Star, and must set off on urgent business. They all now pretended to call his skill in question. This roused his pride, and he thought another half hour could break no squares.[1] Smiler had now had a good feed of corn, and he would only have to push her on a little more; so to it he went.

He won the first game. This spurred him on; and he played till it was so dark they could not see a ball. Another bowl was called for from the winner. Wagers and bets now drained Brown not only of all the money he had won, but of all he had in his pocket, so that he was obliged to ask leave to go to the house where his horse was, to borrow enough to discharge his reckoning at the Globe.

All these losses brought his poor dear mother to his mind, and he marched off with rather a heavy heart to borrow the money, and to order Smiler out of the stable. The landlord expressed much surprise at seeing him, and the ostler[2] declared there was no Smiler there; that she had been rode off above two hours ago by the Merry Andrew, who said he came by order of the owner, Mr. Brown, to fetch her to the Globe, and to pay for the feed. It was indeed one of the neatest

1 Break no squares—to create no trouble.

2 Ostler—or hosteler; a person who takes care of horses.

tricks the Andrew ever performed, for he made such a clean conveyance of Smiler, that neither Jack nor his father ever heard of her again.

It was night; no one could tell what road the Andrew took, and it was another hour or two before an advertisement could be drawn up for apprehending the horse-stealer. Jack had some doubts whether he should go on or return back. He knew that though his father might fear his wife most, yet he loved Smiler best. At length he took that courage from a glass of brandy which he ought to have taken from a hearty repentance, and he resolved to pursue his journey. He was obliged to leave his watch and silver buckles in pawn for a little old hack, which was nothing but skin and bone, and would hardly trot three miles an hour.

He knocked at his father's door about five in the morning. The family were all up. He asked the boy who opened the door how his mother was. "She is dead," said the boy; "she died yesterday afternoon."

Here Jack's heart smote him, and he cried aloud, partly from grief, but more from the reproaches of his own conscience; for he found by computing the hours, that had he come straight on, he should have been in time to receive his mother's blessing.

The father now called from within, "I hear Smiler's step. Is Jack come?"

"Yes, father," said Jack, in a low voice.

"Then," cried the farmer, "run, every man

and boy of you, and take care of the mare. Tom, do thou go and rub her down; Jem, run and get her a good feed of corn. Be sure to walk her about, that she may not catch cold."

Young Brown came in. "Are you not an undutiful dog?" said the father; "you might have been here twelve hours ago. Your mother could not die in peace without seeing you. She said it was a cruel return for all her fondness, that you could not make a little haste to see her; but it was always so, for she had wronged her other children to help you, and this was her reward."

Brown sobbed out a few words, but his father replied, "Never cry, Jack, for the boy told me that it was out of regard for Smiler that you were not here as soon as he was; and if 'twas your over care of her, why there's no great harm done. You could not have saved your poor mother, and you might have hurt the mare."

Here Jack's double guilt flew into his face. He knew that his father was very covetous, and had lived on bad terms with his wife; and also that his own unkindness to her had been forgiven by him out of love to the horse; but to break to him how he had lost that horse through his own folly and want of feeling, was more than Jack had courage to do. The old man, however, soon got at the truth, and no words can describe his fury. Forgetting that his wife lay dead above stairs, he abused his son in a way not fit to be repeated; and though his covetousness had just before found an excuse for a favorite son neglecting to visit a dying parent, yet he now vented his rage against Jack as an unnatural brute, whom he would cut off with a shilling, and bade him never see his face again.

Jack was not allowed to attend his mother's funeral, which was a real grief to him; nor would his father advance even the little money which was needful to redeem his things at the Star. He had now no fond mother to assist him, and he set out on his return home on his borrowed hack, full of grief. He had the additional mortification of knowing, that he had also lost by his folly a little hoard of money which his mother had saved up for him.

When Brown got back to his own town he found that the story of Smiler and the Andrew had got thither before him, and it was thought a very good joke at the Greyhound. He soon recovered his spirits as far as related to the horse; but as to his behavior to his dying mother, it troubled him at times to the last day of his life, though he did all he could to forget it. He did not, however, go on at all the better, nor did he engage in one frolic the less for what had passed at the Globe; his *good heart* continually betraying him into acts of levity and vanity.

Jack began at length to feel the reverse of that proverb, "Keep your shop, and your shop will keep you." He had neglected his customers, and they forsook him. Quarter-day came round; there was much to pay, and little to receive. He owed two years' rent. He was in arrears to his men for wages. He had a long account with his currier.[1] It was in vain to apply to his father. He had now no mother.

Stock was the only true friend he had in the world, and had helped him out of many petty scrapes, but he knew Stock would advance no money in so hopeless a case. Duns came fast about him. He named a speedy day for payment, but as soon as they were out of the house, and the danger put off to a little distance, he forgot every promise, was as merry as ever, and ran the same round of thoughtless gayety. Whenever he was in trouble Stock did not shun him, because that was the moment, he thought, to throw in a little good advice. He one day asked him if he always intended to go on in this course.

"No," said he, "I am resolved by-and-by to reform, grow sober, and go to church. Why, I am but five and twenty, man; I am stout and healthy, and likely to live long; I can repent, and grow melancholy and good at any time."

"O, Jack!" said Stock, "don't cheat thyself with that false hope. What thou dost intend to do, do quickly. Didst thou never read about the heart growing hardened by long indulgence in sin? Some folks, who pretend to mean well, show that they mean nothing at all, by never beginning to put their good resolutions into practice; which made a wise man once say that hell is paved with good intentions. We cannot repent

1 Currier—a man who works with leather.

when we please. 'It is the goodness of God which leadeth us to repentance.' "[1]

"I am sure," replied Jack, "I am no one's enemy but my own."

"It is foolish," said Stock, "to say a bad man is no one's enemy but his own, as that a good man is no one's friend but his own. There is no such neutral character. A bad man corrupts or offends all within reach of his example, just as a good man benefits or instructs all within the sphere of his influence. And there is no time when we can say that this transmitted good and evil will end. A wicked man may be punished for sins he never committed himself, if he has been the cause of sin in others, as surely as a saint will be rewarded for more good deeds than he himself has done, even for the virtues and good actions of all those who are made better by his instruction, his example, or his writings."

Michaelmas-day[2] was at hand. The landlord declared he would be put off no longer, but would seize for rent if it was not paid him on that day, as well as for a considerable sum due to him for leather. Brown now began to be frightened. He applied to Stock to be bound for him. This, Stock flatly refused. Brown now began to dread the horrors of a jail, and really seemed so very contrite, and made so many vows and promises of amendment, that at length Stock was prevailed

1 Romans 2:4—Or despisest thou the riches of his goodness and forbearance and longsuffering; not knowing that the goodness of God leadeth thee to repentance?

2 Michaelmas—a church festival on the 29th of September.

on, together with two or three of Brown's other friends, to advance each a small sum of money to quiet the landlord; Brown promising to make over to them every part of his stock, and to be guided in future by their advice, declaring that he would turn over a new leaf, and follow Mr. Stock's example, as well as his direction in every thing.

Stock's good-nature was at last wrought upon, and he raised the money. The truth is, he did not know the worst, nor how deeply Brown was involved; Brown joyfully set out on the very quarter-day to a town at some distance, to carry his landlord the money, raised by the imprudent kindness of his friend. At his departure Stock put him in mind of the old story of Smiler and the Merry Andrew, and he promised of his own head that he would not even call at a public-house till he had paid the money.

He was as good as his word. He very triumphantly passed by several. He stopped a little under the window of one where the sounds of merriment and loud laughter caught his ear. At another he heard the enticing notes of a fiddle and the light heels of the merry dancers. Here his heart had well-nigh failed him, but the dread of a jail on the one hand, and what he feared almost as much, Mr. Stock's anger on the other, spurred him on; and he valued himself not a little at having got the better of this temptation. He felt quite happy when he found he had reached the door of his landlord without having yielded to one idle inclination.

He knocked at the door. The maid who opened it said her master was not at home.

"I am sorry for it," said he, strutting about, and with a boasting air he took out his money. "I want to pay him my rent: he need not have been afraid of me."

The servant, who knew her master was very much afraid of him, desired him to walk in, for her master would be at home in half an hour.

"I will call again," said he; "but no, let him call on me, and the sooner the better: I shall be at the Blue Posts."

While he had been talking he took care to open his black leather case, and to display the bank-bills to the servant, and then, in a swaggering way, he put up his money and marched off to the Blue Posts.

He was by this time quite proud of his own resolution, and having tendered the money, and being clear in his own mind that it was the landlord's own fault, and not his, that it was not paid, he went to refresh himself at the Blue Posts.

In a barn belonging to this public-house some strollers were just going to perform some of that sing-song ribaldry by which our villages are corrupted, the laws broken, and that money drawn from the poor for pleasure, which is wanted by their families for bread. The name of the last new song which made part of the entertainment, made him think himself in high luck, that he should have just that half hour to spare.

He went into the barn, but was too much delighted with the actor, who sung his favorite song, to remain a quiet hearer. He leaped out of the pit, and got behind the two ragged blankets which served for a curtain. He sung so much better than the actors themselves, that they praised and admired him to a degree which awakened all his vanity. He was so intoxicated with their flattery, that he could do no less than invite them all to supper, an invitation which they were too hungry not to accept.

He did not, however, quite forget his appointment with his landlord; but the half hour was long since passed by. "And so," says he, "as I know he is a mean curmudgeon, who goes to bed I suppose by daylight, to save candle, it will be too late to speak with him tonight, besides, let him call upon me; it is his business, and not mine. I left word where I was to be found; the money is ready, and if I don't pay him tonight, I can do it before breakfast."

By the time these firm resolutions were made, supper was ready. There never was a more jolly evening; ale and punch were as plenty as water. The actors saw what a vain fellow was feasting them; and as they wanted victuals, and he wanted flattery, the business was soon settled. They ate, and Brown sung. They pretended to be in raptures. Singing promoted drinking, and every fresh glass produced a song, or a story, still more merry than the former. Before morning, the players, who were engaged to act in another barn a dozen miles off, stole away quietly. Brown having dropped asleep, they left him to finish his nap by himself. As to him, his dreams were gay and pleasant, and the house being quite still, he slept comfortably till morning.

As soon as he had breakfasted, the business of the night before popped into his head. He set off once more to his landlord's in high spirits, gayly singing by the way scraps of all the tunes he had picked up the night before from his new friends. The landlord opened the door himself, and reproached him with no small surliness for not having kept his word with him the evening before, adding, that he supposed he was come now with some more of his shallow excuses. Brown put on all that haughtiness which is common to people who being generally apt to be in the wrong, happen to catch themselves doing a right action; and he looked big, as some sort of people do, when they have money to pay.

"You need not have been so anxious about your money," said he; "I was not going to break or run away." The landlord knew this was the common language of those who are ready to do both. Brown haughtily added, "You shall see I am a man of my word; give me a receipt." The landlord had it ready, and gave it him.

Brown put his hand in his pocket for his black leather case in which the bills were; he felt, he searched, he examined first one pocket, then the other, then both waistcoat pockets, but no leather case could he find. He looked terrified. It was the face of real terror, but the landlord conceived it to be that of guilt, and abused him heartily for putting his old tricks upon him; he swore he would not be imposed upon any longer—the money or a jail, there lay his choice.

Brown protested for once with great truth, that he had no intention to deceive; declared that he had actually brought the money, and knew not what had become of it; but the thing was far too unlikely to gain credit. Brown now called to mind that he had fallen asleep on the settle in the room where they had supped. This raised his spirits, for he had no doubt but the case had fallen out of his pocket; he said he would step to the public-house and search for it, and would be back directly. Not one word of all this did the landlord believe, so inconvenient is it to have a bad character. He swore Brown should not stir out of his house without a constable, and made him wait while he sent for one. Brown, guarded by the constable, went back to the Blue Posts, the landlord charging the officer not to lose sight of the culprit. The caution was needless; Brown had not the least design of running away, so firmly persuaded was he that he should find his leather ease.

But who can paint his dismay, when no tale or tidings of the leather case could be had! The master, the mistress, the boy, and the maid of the public-house all protested they were innocent. His suspicion soon fell on the strollers with whom he had passed the night; and he now found out, for the first time, that a merry evening did not always produce a happy morning. He obtained a warrant, and proper officers were sent in pursuit of the strollers. No one, however, believed he had really lost any thing; and as he had not a shilling left to defray the expensive treat he had given, the master of the inn agreed with the other landlord in thinking this story was a trick to defraud them both, and Brown remained in close custody.

At length the officers returned, who said they had been obliged to let the strollers go, as they could not fix the charge on any one, and they had all offered to swear before a justice that they had seen nothing of the leather case. It was at length agreed, that as he had passed the evening in a crowded barn, he had probably been robbed there, if at all; and among so many, who could pretend to guess at the thief?

Brown raved like a madman; he cried, tore his hair, and said he was ruined for ever. The abusive language of his old landlord, and his new creditor at the Blue Posts, did not lighten his sorrow. His landlord would be put off no longer. Brown declared he could neither find bail, nor raise another shilling, and as soon as the forms of law were made out, he was sent to the county jail.

Here it might have been expected that hard living and much leisure would bring him to reflect a little on his past follies. But his heart was not truly touched. The chief thing which grieved him at first was, his having abused the kindness of Stock, for to him he should appear guilty of a real fraud, where he had indeed been only vain, idle, and imprudent. And it is worth while here to remark, that vanity, idleness, and imprudence, often bring a man to ruin both soul and body, though silly people do not put them in the catalogue of heavy sins, and those who indulge in them are often reckoned honest, merry fellows, with *the best hearts in the world.*

In the fourth part my readers will know what befell Jack in his present doleful habitation, and what became of him afterwards.

PART IV

JACK BROWN IN PRISON

BROWN was no sooner lodged in his doleful habitation, and a little recovered from his first surprise, than he sat down and wrote to his friend Stock the whole history of the transaction. Mr. Stock, who had long known the exceeding lightness and dissipation of his mind, did not so utterly disbelieve the story as all the other creditors did. To speak the truth, Stock was the only one among them who had good sense enough to know that a man may be completely ruined, both in what relates to his property and his soul, without committing Old Bailey[1] crimes. He well knew that idleness, vanity, and the love of *pleasure*, as it is falsely called, will bring a man to a morsel of bread as surely as those things which are reckoned much greater sins; and that they undermine his principles as certainly, though not perhaps quite so fast.

Stock was too angry at what had happened to answer Brown's letter, or to seem to take the least notice of him. However, he kindly and

1 Old Bailey—a criminal court in London for serious crimes.

secretly undertook a journey to the hardhearted old farmer, Brown's father, to intercede with him, and to see if he would do any thing for his son. Stock did not pretend to excuse Jack, or even to lessen his offences; for it was a rule of his, never to disguise truth or to palliate wickedness. Sin was still sin in his eyes, though it were committed by his best friend; but though he would not soften the sin, he felt tenderly for the sinner. He pleaded with the old farmer on the ground that his son's idleness and other vices would gather fresh strength in a jail. He told him, that the loose and worthless company which he would there keep would harden him in vice, and if he was now wicked, he might there become irreclaimable.

But all his pleas were urged in vain. The farmer was not to be moved. Indeed he argued, with some justice, that he ought not to make his industrious children beggars to save one rogue from the gallows. Mr. Stock allowed the force of his reasoning, though he saw the father was less influenced by this principle of justice than by resentment on account of the old story of Smiler. People, indeed, should take care that what appears in their conduct to proceed from justice, does not really proceed from revenge. Wiser men than farmer Brown often deceive themselves, and fancy they act on better principles than they really do, for want of looking a little more closely into their own hearts, and putting down every action to its true motive.

When we are praying against deceit, we should not forget to take self-deceit into the account.

Mr. Stock at length wrote to poor Jack, not to offer him any help, that was quite out of the question, but to exhort him to repent of his evil ways; to lay before him the sins of his past life, and to advise him to convert the present punishment into a benefit, by humbling himself before God. He offered his interest to get his place of confinement exchanged for one of those improved prisons, where solitude and labor have been made the happy instruments of bringing many to a better way of thinking; and ended by saying, that if he ever gave any solid signs of real amendment he would still be his friend, in spite of all that was past.

If Mr. Stock had sent him a good sum of money to procure his liberty, or even a trifle to make merry with his wretched companions, Jack would have thought him a friend indeed. But to send him nothing but dry advice, and a few words of empty comfort, was, he thought, but a cheap, shabby way of showing his kindness. Unluckily, the letter came just as he was going to sit down to one of those direful merry-makings which are often carried on with brutal riot within the doleful walls of a jail on the entrance of a new prisoner, who is often expected to give a feast to the rest.

When his companions were heated with gin, "Now," said Jack, "I'll treat you with a sermon, and a very pretty preachment it is." So saying,

"I'LL TREAT YOU WITH A SERMON," JACK SAID.

he took out Mr. Stock's kind and pious letter, and was delighted at the bursts of laughter it produced.

"What a canting dog," said one.

"Repentance, indeed," cried Tom Crew; "no, no, Jack, tell this hypocritical rogue that if we have lost our liberty, it is only for having been jolly, hearty fellows, and we have more spirit than to repent of that, I hope; all the harm we have done is living a little too fast, like honest bucks as we are."

"Aye, aye," said Jolly George, "had we been such sneaking, miserly fellows as Stock, we need not have come hither. But if the ill-nature of the laws has been so cruel as to clap up such fine hearty blades, we are no *felons* however. We are afraid of no Jack Ketch; and I see no cause to repent of any sin that's not hanging-matter. As to those who are thrust into the condemned hole indeed, and have but a few hours to live, they *must* see the parson, and hear a sermon, and such stuff. But I do not know what such stout young fellows as we are have to do with repentance. And so, Jack, let us have that rare new catch which you learnt of the strollers that merry night when you lost your pocket-book."

This thoughtless youth soon gave a fresh proof of the power of evil company, and of the quick progress of the heart of a sinner from bad to worse. Brown, who always wanted principle, soon grew to want feeling also. He joined in the laugh which was raised against Stock, and told many *good stories,* as they were called, in derision of the piety, sobriety, and self-denial of his old friend. He lost every day somewhat of those small remains of shame and decency which he had brought with him to the prison. He even grew reconciled to this wretched way of life, and the want of money seemed to him the heaviest evil in the life of a jail.

Mr. Stock finding, from the jailer, that his letter had been treated with ridicule, would not write to him any more. He did not come to see him, nor send him any assistance, thinking it right to let him suffer that want which his vices had brought upon him. But, as he still hoped that the time would come when he might be brought to a sense of his own evil courses, he continued to have an eye upon him by means of the jailer, who was an honest, kindhearted man.

Brown spent one part of his time in thoughtless rioting, and the other in gloomy sadness. Company kept up his spirits; with his new friends he contrived to drown thought; but when he was alone he began to find that a *merry fellow,* when deprived of his companions and his liquor, is often a most forlorn wretch. Then it is, that even a merry fellow says "of laughter, What is it? and of mirth, It is madness."

As he contrived, however, to be as little alone as possible, his gayety was commonly uppermost, till that loathsome distemper called the jail-fever broke out in the prison. Tom Crew, the ringleader in all their evil practices, was first seized with it. Jack stayed a little while with his comrade to assist and divert him, but of assistance he could give little, and the very thought of diversion was now turned into horror. He soon caught the distemper, and that in so dreadful a degree that his life was in great danger. Of those who remained in health not a soul came near him, though he had shared his last farthing with them. He had just sense enough left to feel this cruelty.

Poor fellow! he did not know before, that the friendship of the worldly is at an end when there is no more drink or diversion to be had. He lay in the most deplorable condition; his body tormented with a dreadful disease, and his soul terrified and amazed at the approach of death—that death which he thought at so great a distance, and of which his comrades had assured him that a young fellow of five-and-twenty was in no danger. Poor Jack! I cannot help feeling for him. Without a shilling! without a friend! without one comfort respecting this world, and, what is far more terrible, without one hope respecting the next!

Let not the young reader fancy that Brown's misery arose entirely from his altered circumstances. It was not merely his being in want, and sick, and in prison, which made his condition so desperate. Many an honest man unjustly accused, many a persecuted saint, many a holy martyr, has enjoyed sometimes more peace and content in a prison, than wicked men have ever tasted in the height of their prosperity. But to any such comforts, to any comfort at all, poor Jack was an utter stranger.

A Christian friend generally comes forward at the very time when worldly friends forsake the wretched. The other prisoners would not come near Brown, though he had often entertained and never offended them; even his own father was not moved with his sad condition. When Mr. Stock informed him of it, he answered, " 'Tis no more than he deserves. 'As he brews, so he must bake.' 'He has made his own bed, and let him lie in it.' "

The hard old man had ever at his tongue's end some proverb of hardness or frugality, which he contrived to turn in such a way as to excuse himself.

We shall now see how Mr. Stock behaved. He had his favorite sayings too, but they were chiefly on the side of kindness, mercy, or some other virtue. "I must not," said he, "pretend to call myself a Christian, if I do not requite evil with good."

When he received the jailer's letter with the account of Brown's sad condition, Will Simpson and Tommy Williams began to compliment him on his own wisdom and prudence, by which he had escaped Brown's misfortunes. He only gravely said, "Blessed be God, that I am not in the same misery. It is *He* who has made us to differ. But for *His* grace I might have been in no better condition. Now Brown is brought low by the hand of God, it is my time to go to him."

"What, you!" said Will, "whom he cheated of your money?"

"This is not a time to remember injuries," said Mr. Stock; "how can I ask forgiveness for my own sins, if I withhold forgiveness from him?"

So saying, he ordered his horse, and set off to see poor Brown; thus proving that his was a religion not of words, but of deeds.

Stock's heart nearly failed him as he passed through the prison. The groans of the sick and dying, and what to such a heart as his was still more moving, the brutal merriment of the healthy in such a place, pierced his very soul. Many a silent prayer did he put up as he passed along, that God would yet be pleased to touch their hearts, and that now, during this infectious sickness, might be the accepted time. The jailer observed him drop a tear, and asked the cause.

"I cannot forget," said he, "that the most dissolute of these men is still my fellow-creature. The same God made them; the same Savior died for them; how then can I hate the worst of them? With my advantages, they might have been much better than I am; without the blessing of God on my good minister's instructions, I might have been worse than the worst of these. I have no cause for pride, much for thankfulness. 'Let us not be high-minded, but fear.' "

It would have moved a heart of stone to see poor miserable Jack Brown lying on his wretched bed, his face so changed by pain, poverty, dirt, and sorrow, that he could hardly be known for that merry soul of a jack-boot, as he used to be proud to hear himself called. His groans were so piteous that it made Mr. Stock's heart ache. He kindly took him by the hand, though he knew the distemper was catching.

"How dost do, Jack?" said he: "dost know me?"

Brown shook his head, and said faintly, "Know you? aye, that I do. I am sure I have but one friend in the world who would come to see me in this woeful condition. O, James! what have I brought myself to? What will become of my poor soul? I dare not look back, for that is all sin; nor forward, for that is all misery and woe."

Mr. Stock spoke kindly to him, but did not attempt to cheer him with false comfort, as is too often done.

"I am ashamed to see you in this dirty place," says Brown.

"As to the place, Jack," replied the other, "if it has helped to bring you to a sense of your past offences, it will be no bad place for you. I am heartily sorry for your distress and your sickness; but if it should please God by them to open your eyes, and to show you that sin is a greater evil than the prison to which it has brought you, all may yet be well. I had rather see you in this humble, penitent state, lying on this dirty bed, in this dismal prison, than roaring and rioting at the Greyhound, the king of the company, with handsome clothes on your back, and plenty of money in your pocket."

Brown wept bitterly, and squeezed his hand, but was too weak to say much. Mr. Stock then desired the jailer to let him have such things as were needful, and he would pay for them. He would not leave the poor fellow till he had given him with his own hands some broth which the jailer had got ready for him, and some medicines which the doctor had sent.

All this kindness cut Brown to the heart. He was just able to sob out, "My unnatural father leaves me to perish, and my injured friend is more than a father to me."

Stock told him that one proof he must give of his repentance was, that he must forgive his father, whose provocation had been very great. He then said he would leave him for the present to take some rest, and desired him to lift up his heart to God for mercy.

"Dear James," replied Brown, "do you pray for me? God perhaps may hear you, but he will never hear the prayer of such a sinner as I have been."

"Take care how you think so," said Stock. "To believe that God cannot forgive you, would be still a greater sin than any you have yet committed against him." He then explained to him in a few words, as well as he was able, the nature of repentance, and forgiveness through a Savior, and warned him earnestly against unbelief and hardness of heart.

Poor Jack grew much refreshed in body with the comfortable things he had taken, and a little cheered with Stock's kindness in coming so far to see and to forgive such a forlorn outcast, sick of an infectious distemper, and locked within the walls of a prison. Surely, said he to himself, there must be some mighty power in a religion which can lead men to do such things—things so much against the grain as to forgive such an injury, and to risk catching such a distemper; but he was so weak he could not express this in words. He tried to pray, but he could not; at length, overpowered with weariness, he fell asleep.

When Mr. Stock came back, he was surprised to find him so much better in body; but his agonies of mind were dreadful, and he had now got strength to express part of the horrors which he felt.

"James," said he, looking wildly, "it is all over with me. I am a lost creature. Even your prayers cannot save me."

"Dear Jack," replied Mr. Stock, "I am no minister, but I know I may venture to say whatever is in the Bible. As ignorant as I am, I shall be safe enough while I stick to that."

"Aye," said the sick man, "you used to be ready enough to read to me, and I would not listen, or if I did, it was only to make fun of what I heard, and now you will not so much as read a bit of a chapter to me."

This was the very point to which Stock longed to bring him. So he took a little Bible out of his pocket, which he always carried with him on a journey, and read slowly, verse by verse, the fifty-fifth chapter of Isaiah. When he came to the sixth and seventh verses, poor Jack cried so much that Stock was forced to stop. The words were, "Let the wicked forsake his way, and the unrighteous man his thoughts, and let him return unto the Lord." Here Brown stopped him, saying, "O, it is too late, too late for me."

"Let me finish the verse," said Stock, "and you will see your error; you will see that it is never too late." So he read on: "Let him return unto the Lord, and he will have mercy upon him; and to our God, for he will abundantly pardon."

Here Brown started up, snatched the book out of his hand, and cried out, "Is that really there? No, no; that's of your own putting in, in order to comfort me; let me look at the words myself."

"No, indeed," said Stock, "I would not for the world give you unfounded comfort, or put off any notion of my own for a scripture doctrine."

"But is it possible," cried the sick man, "that God may really pardon me? Dost think he can? Dost think he will?"

"I am sure of it," said Stock; "I dare not give thee false hopes, or indeed any hopes of my own. But these are God's own words, and the only difficulty is, to know when we are really brought into such a state as that the words may be applied to us; for a text may be full of comfort, and yet not belong to us."

Mr. Stock was afraid of saying more. He

WHEN HE CAME TO THE SIXTH AND SEVENTH VERSES,
POOR JACK CRIED.

would not venture out of his depth; nor, indeed, was poor Brown able to bear more discourse just now. So he made him a present of the Bible, folding down such places as he thought might be best suited to his state, and took his leave, being obliged to return home that night. He left a little money with the jailer, to add a few comforts to the allowance of the prison, and promised to return in a short time.

When he got home, he described the sufferings and misery of Brown in a very moving manner; but Tommy Williams, instead of being properly affected at it, only said, "Indeed, master, I am not very sorry; he is rightly served."

"How, Tommy," said Mr. Stock, rather sternly "not sorry to see a fellow-creature brought to the lowest state of misery? one too whom you have known so prosperous?"

"No, master, I can't say I am; for Mr. Brown used to make fun of you, and laugh at you for being so godly, and reading your Bible."

"Let me say a few words to you, Tommy," said Mr. Stock. "In the first place, you should never watch for the time of a man's being brought low by trouble, to tell of his faults. Next, you should never rejoice at his trouble, but pity him, and pray for him. Lastly, as to his ridiculing me for my religion, if I cannot stand an idle jest, I am not worthy the name of a Christian. 'He that is ashamed of me and my words'—dost remember what follows, Tommy?"

"Yes, master, 'twas last Sunday's text: of him

shall the Son of man be ashamed when he shall judge the world.' "[1]

Mr. Stock soon went back to the prison. But he did not go alone. He took with him Mr. Thomas, the worthy minister who had been the guide and instructor of his youth, who was so kind as to go at his request, and visit this forlorn prisoner.

When they got to Brown's door, they found him sitting up in his bed with the Bible in his hand. This was a joyful sight to Mr. Stock, who secretly thanked God for it. Brown was reading aloud; they listened; it was the fifteenth of St. Luke. The circumstances of this beautiful parable of the prodigal son were so much like his own, that the story pierced him to the soul; and he stopped every minute to compare his own case with that of the prodigal. He had just got to the eighteenth verse, "I will arise, and go to my father"—at that moment he spied his two friends; joy darted into his eyes.

"O, dear Jem," said he, "it is *not* too late; I will arise, and go to my Father, my heavenly Father; and you, sir, will show me the way, wont you?" said he to Mr. Thomas, whom he recollected.

"I am very glad to see you in so hopeful a disposition," said the good minister.

"O, sir," said Brown, "what a place is this to

1 Mark 8:38—Whosoever therefore shall be ashamed of me and of my words in this adulterous and sinful generation; of him also shall the Son of man be ashamed, when he cometh in the glory of his Father with the holy angels.

receive you in! O, see to what I have brought myself!"

"Your condition, as to this world, is indeed very low," replied the good pastor. "But what are mines, dungeons, or galleys, to that eternal, hopeless prison, to which your unrepented sins must soon have consigned you? Even in this gloomy prison, on this bed of straw, worn down by pain, poverty, and want, forsaken by your worldly friends, an object of scorn to those with whom you used to carouse and riot; yet here, I say, brought thus low, if you have at last found out your own vileness, and your utterly undone state by sin, you may still be more an object of favor in the sight of God, than when you thought yourself prosperous and happy—when the world smiled upon you, and you passed your days and nights in envied gayety and unchristian riot.

"If you will but improve the present awful visitation; if you do but heartily renounce and abhor your present evil courses; if you even now turn to the Lord your Savior with lively faith, deep repentance, and unfeigned obedience, I shall still have more hope of you than of many who are going on quite happy, because quite insensible. The heavy laden sinner, who has discovered the iniquity of his own heart, and his utter inability to help himself, may be restored to God's favor, and become happy, though in a dungeon. And be assured, that he who, from deep and humble contrition, dares not so much as to lift up his eyes to heaven, when with a hearty faith he sighs out, 'God, be merciful to me a sinner,'[1] shall in no wise be cast out. These are the words of Him who cannot lie."

It is impossible to describe the self-abasement, the grief, the joy, the shame, the hope, and the fear which filled the mind of this poor man. A dawn of comfort at length shone on his benighted mind. His humility and fear of falling back into his former sins, if he should ever recover, Mr. Thomas thought were strong symptoms of a sound repentance. He improved and cherished every right feeling he saw rising in his heart, and particularly warned him against self-deceit, self-confidence, and hypocrisy.

After Brown had deeply expressed his sorrow for his offenses, Mr. Thomas thus addressed him:—"There are two ways to be sorry for sin. Are you, Mr. Brown, afraid of the guilt of sin because of the punishment annexed to it, or are you afraid of sin itself? Do you wish to be delivered from the power of sin? do you hate sin because you know it is offensive to a pure and holy God? or are you only ashamed of it because it has brought you to a prison, and exposed you to the contempt of the world? It is not said that the wages of this or that particular sin is death, but of sin in general; there is no exception made because it is more creditable, or a favorite sin, or because it is a little one. There are, I repeat, two ways of being sorry for sin. Cain was sorry—'My

1 Luke 18:13—And the publican, standing afar off, would not lift up so much as his eyes unto heaven, but smote upon his breast, saying, God be merciful to me a sinner.

punishment is greater than I can bear,'[1] said he; but here you see the punishment seemed to be the cause of concern, not of sin. David seems to have had a true notion of godly sorrow, when he says, 'Wash me from mine iniquity, cleanse me from my sin.'[2] And when Job 'repented in dust and ashes,' it is not said he excused himself, but 'he abhorred himself.'[3] And the prophet Isaiah called himself 'undone,' because he was 'a man of unclean lips;' for, said he, 'I have seen the King, the Lord of hosts;'[4] that is, he could not take the proper measure of his own iniquity till he had considered the perfect holiness of God."

One day, when Mr. Thomas and Mr. Stock came to see him, they found him more than commonly affected. His face was more ghastly pale than usual, and his eyes were red with crying.

"Oh, sir," said he, "what a sight have I just seen! Jolly George, as we used to call him, the ringleader of all our mirth, who was at the bottom of all the fun, and tricks, and wickedness, that are carried on within these walls—Jolly George is just dead of the jail-distemper! He taken, and I left! I *would* be carried into his room to speak to him, to beg him to take warning by me, and that I might take warning by him. But

---

1 Genesis 4:13—And Cain said unto the LORD, My punishment is greater than I can bear.

2 Psalm 51:2—Wash me thoroughly from mine iniquity, and cleanse me from my sin.

3 Job 42:6—Wherefore I abhor myself, and repent in dust and ashes.

4 Isaiah 6:5—Then said I, Woe is me! for I am undone; because I am a man of unclean lips, and I dwell in the midst of a people of unclean lips: for mine eyes have seen the King, the LORD of hosts.

what did I see? What did I hear? Not one sign of repentance; not one dawn of hope. Agony of body, blasphemies on his tongue, despair in his soul; while I am spared and comforted with hopes of mercy and acceptance. O, if all my old friends at the Greyhound could but then have seen Jolly George! A hundred sermons about death, sir, don't speak so home, and cut so deep, as the sight of one dying sinner."

Brown grew gradually better in his health, that is, the fever mended, but the distemper settled in his limbs, so that he seemed likely to be a poor weakly cripple the rest of his life. But as he spent much of his time in prayer, and in reading such parts of the Bible as Mr. Thomas directed, he improved every day in knowledge and piety, and of course grew more resigned to pain and infirmity.

Some months after this, his hard-hearted father, who had never been prevailed upon to see him, or offer him the least relief, was taken off suddenly by a fit of apoplexy; and, after all his threatenings, he died without a will. He was one of those silly, superstitious men, who fancy they shall die the sooner for having made one; and who love the world and the things that are in the world so dearly, that they dread to set about any business which may put them in mind that they are not always to live in it.

As, by this neglect, his father had not fulfilled his threat of cutting him off with a shilling, Jack, of course, went shares with his brothers in what their father left. What fell to him proved to be just enough to discharge him from prison, and to pay all his debts, but he had nothing left. His joy at being thus able to make restitution was so great, that he thought little of his own wants. He did not desire to conceal the most trifling debt, nor to keep a shilling for himself.

Mr. Stock undertook to settle all his affairs. There did not remain money enough, after every creditor was satisfied, even to pay for his removal home. Mr. Stock kindly sent his own cart for him with a bed in it, made as comfortable as possible, for he was too weak and lame to be removed any other way; and Mrs. Stock gave the driver a particular charge to be tender and careful of him, and not to drive hard, nor to leave the cart a moment.

Mr. Stock would fain have taken him into his own house, at least for a time, so convinced was he of his sincere reformation, both in heart and life; but Brown would not be prevailed on to be further burdensome to this generous friend. He insisted on being carried to the parish workhouse, which he said was a far better place than he deserved. In this house Mr. Stock furnished a small room for him, and sent him every day a morsel of meat from his own dinner. Tommy Williams begged that he might always be allowed to carry it, as some atonement for his having for a moment so far forgotten his duty, as rather to rejoice than sympathize in Brown's misfortunes. He never thought of this fault without sorrow, and often thanked his master for the wholesome lesson he then gave him; and he was the better for it all his life.

Mrs. Stock often carried poor Brown a bit of tea or a basin of good broth herself. He was quite a cripple, and never able to walk out as long as he lived. Mr. Stock, Will Simpson, and Tommy Williams laid their heads together, and contrived a sort of barrow, on which he was often carried to church by some of his poor neighbors, of which Tommy was always one; and he requited their kindness by reading a good book to them whenever they would call in, or teaching their children to sing psalms or say the catechism.

It was no small joy to him thus to be enabled to go to church. Whenever he was carried by the Greyhound, he was much moved, and used to put up a prayer full of repentance for the past, and praise for the present.

PART V

A DIALOGUE BETWEEN JAMES STOCK AND WILL SIMPSON, THE SHOEMAKERS, AS THEY SAT AT WORK, ON THE DUTY OF CARRYING RELIGION INTO OUR COMMON BUSINESS

JAMES STOCK and his journeyman, Will Simpson, as I informed my readers in the second part, had resolved to work together one hour every evening, in order to pay for Tommy Williams' schooling. This circumstance brought them to be a good deal together when the rest of the men were gone home. Now, it happened that Mr. Stock had a pleasant way of endeavoring to turn all common events to some use; and he thought it right on the present occasion to make the only return in his power to Will Simpson for his great kindness. "For," said he, "if Will gives up so much of his time to help me to provide for this poor boy, it is the least I can do to try to turn part of that time to the purpose of promoting Will's spiritual good."

Now, as the bent of Stock's own mind was religious, it was easy to him to lead their talk to something profitable. He always took especial care, however, that the subject should be introduced properly, cheerfully, and without constraint. As he well knew that great good may be sometimes done by a prudent attention in seizing proper opportunities, so he knew that the cause of piety had been sometimes hurt by forcing serious subjects where there was clearly no disposition to receive them. I say he had found out that two things were necessary to the promoting of true religion among his friends; a warm zeal to be always on the watch for occasions, and a cool judgment to distinguish which was the right time and place to make use of them. To know *how* to do good, is a great matter; but to know *when* to do it, is no small one.

Simpson was an honest, good-natured man; he was now become sober, and rather religiously disposed. But he was ignorant; he did not know much of the grounds of religion, or of the corruption of his own nature; he was regular at church, but was first drawn thither rather by his skill in psalm-singing than by any great devotion. He had left off going to the Greyhound, and often read the Bible, or some other good book, on Sunday evening. This he thought was quite enough. He thought the Bible was the prettiest history-book in the world, and that religion was a very good thing for Sundays; but he did not much understand what business people had with it on working days.

He had left off drinking because it had

brought Williams to the grave, and his wife to dirt and rags; but not because he himself had seen the evil of sin. He now considered swearing and Sabbath-breaking as scandalous and indecent, but he had not found out that both were to be left off because they are highly offensive to God, and grieve his Holy Spirit.

As Simpson was less self-conceited than most ignorant people are, Stock had always a good hope, that when he should come to be better acquainted with the word of God, and with the evil of his own heart, he would become one day a good Christian. The great hindrance to this was, that he fancied himself so already.

One evening, Simpson had been calling to Stock's mind how disorderly the house and shop, where they were now sitting quietly at work, had formerly been, and he went on thus:—

WILL. How comfortably we live now, master, to what we used to do in Williams' time: I used then never to be happy but when we were keeping it up all night, but now I am as merry as the day is long. I find I am twice as happy since I am grown good and sober.

STOCK. I am glad you are happy, Will, and I rejoice that you are sober; but I would not have you take too much pride in your own *goodness*, for fear it should become a sin almost as great as some of those you have left off. Besides, I would not have you make quite so sure that you *are* good.

WILL. Not good, master! why, don't you find me regular and orderly at work?

STOCK. Very much so, and accordingly I have a great respect for you.

WILL. I pay every one his own, seldom miss church, have not been drunk since Williams died, have handsome clothes for Sundays, and save a trifle every week.

STOCK. Very true, and very laudable it is; and to all this you may add, that you very generously work an hour for poor Tommy's education, every evening, without fee or reward.

WILL. Well, master, what can a man do more? If all this is not being good, I don't know what is.

STOCK. All these things are very right as far as they go; and you could not well be a Christian without doing them. But I shall make you stare, perhaps, when I tell you, you may do all these things, and many more, and yet be no Christian.

WILL. No Christian! Surely, master, I do hope that after all I have done, you will not be so unkind as to say I am no Christian.

STOCK. God forbid that I should say so, Will; I hope better things of you. But come, now, what do you think it is to be a Christian?

WILL. What! why, to be christened when one is a child, to learn the catechism when one can read, to be confirmed when one is a youth, and to go to church when one is a man.

STOCK. These are all very proper things, and quite necessary. They make part of a Christian's life. But, for all that, a man may be exact in them all, and yet not be a Christian.

WILL. Not be a Christian! ha! ha! ha! you are very comical, master.

STOCK. No, indeed, I am very serious, Will. At this rate it would be a very easy thing to be a Christian, and every man who went through certain forms would be a good man; and one man who observed these forms would be as good as another. Whereas, if we examine ourselves by the word of God, I am afraid there are but few, comparatively, whom our Savior would allow to be real Christians. What is your notion of a Christian's practice?

WILL. Why, he must not rob, nor murder, nor get drunk. He must avoid scandalous things, and do as other decent, orderly people do.

STOCK. It is easy enough to be what the world calls a Christian, but not so easy to be what the Bible calls so.

WILL. Why, master, we working men are not expected to be saints, and martyrs, and apostles, and ministers.

STOCK. We are not. And yet, Will, there are not two sorts of Christianity; we are called to practice the same religion which they practiced, and something of the same spirit is expected in us, which we reverence in them. It was not saints and martyrs only to whom our Savior said, that they must 'crucify the world, with its affections and lusts.'[1] We are called to 'be holy' in our measure and degree, 'as He who hath called

1 Galatians 5:24—And they that are Christ's have crucified the flesh with the affections and lusts.

us is holy.'[1] It was not only saints and martyrs who were told that they must be 'like-minded with Christ'—that they must 'do all to the glory of God'[2]—that they must renounce the spirit of the world, and 'deny themselves.' It was not to apostles only that Christ said, their 'conversation must be in heaven.'[3] It was not to a few holy men set apart for the ministry that he said, they must 'set their affections on things above'[4]—that they must 'not be conformed to the world.'[5] No; it was to fishermen, to publicans, to farmers, to day-laborers, to poor tradesmen, that he spoke when he told them they must 'love not the world, nor the things of the world'[6]—that they must 'renounce the hidden things of dishonesty,' 'grow in grace,' 'lay up for themselves treasures in heaven.'[7]

WILL. All this might be very proper for *them* to be taught, because they had not been bred up Christians, but heathens or Jews; and Christ

---

1 1 Peter 1:15–16—But as he which hath called you is holy, so be ye holy in all manner of conversation; Because it is written, Be ye holy; for I am holy.

2 1 Corinthians 10:31—Whether therefore ye eat, or drink, or whatsoever ye do, do all to the glory of God.

3 Philippians 3:20—For our conversation is in heaven; from whence also we look for the Savior, the Lord Jesus Christ.

4 Colossians 3:2—Set your affection on things above, not on things on the earth.

5 Romans 12:2—And be not conformed to this world: but be ye transformed by the renewing of your mind, that ye may prove what is that good, and acceptable, and perfect, will of God.

6 1 John 2:15—Love not the world, neither the things that are in the world. If any man love the world, the love of the Father is not in him.

7 Matthew 6:20—But lay up for yourselves treasures in heaven, where neither moth nor rust doth corrupt, and where thieves do not break through nor steal.

wanted to make them his followers, that is, Christians. But, thank God, we do not want to be taught all this, for we *are* Christians, born in a Christian country, of Christian parents.

STOCK. I suppose, then, you fancy that Christianity comes to people in a Christian country by nature?

WILL. I think it comes by a good education, or a good example. When a fellow who has got any sense sees a man cut off in his prime by drinking, like Williams, I think he will begin to leave it off. When he sees another man respected, like you, master, for honesty and sobriety, and going to church, why, he will grow honest and sober and go to church; that is, he will see it is his advantage to be a Christian.

STOCK. Will, what you say is the truth, but 'tis not the whole truth. You are right as far as you go, but you do not go far enough. The worldly advantages of piety are, as you suppose, in general, great. Credit, prosperity, and health, almost naturally attend on a religious life, both because a religious life supposes a sober and industrious life, and because a man who lives in a course of duty puts himself in the way of God's blessing. But a true Christian has a still higher aim in view, and will follow religion even under circumstances when it may hurt his credit, and ruin his property, if it should ever happen to be the will of God that he should be brought into such a trying state.

WILL. Well, master, to speak the truth, if I

go to church on Sundays, and follow my work in the week, I must say I think that is being good.

STOCK. I agree with you, that he who does both gives the best outward signs that he is good, as you call it. But our going to church, and even reading the Bible, are no proofs that we are as good as we need be, but rather that we do both these in order to make us better than we are. We do both on Sundays as means, by God's blessing, to make us better all the week. We are to bring the fruits of that chapter or of that sermon into our daily life, and try to get our inmost heart and secret thoughts, as well as our daily conduct, amended by them.

WILL. Why, sure, master, you wont be so unreasonable as to want a body to be religious always? I can't do that neither. I'm not such a hypocrite as to pretend to it.

STOCK. Yes, you can be so in every action of your life.

WILL. What, master, always to be thinking about religion?

STOCK. No, far from it, Will; much less to be always talking about it. But you must be always acting under its power and spirit.

WILL. But surely 'tis pretty well if I do this when I go to church, or while I am saying my prayers. Even you, master, as strict as you are, would not have me always on my knees, nor always at church, I suppose; for then how would your work be carried on? and how would our town be supplied with shoes?

STOCK. Very true, Will. 'Twould be no proof of our religion to let our customers go barefoot; but 'twould be a proof of our laziness, and we should starve as we ought to do. The business of the world must not only be carried on, but carried on with spirit and activity. We have the same authority for not being 'slothful in business,' as we have for being 'fervent in spirit.' Religion has put godliness and laziness as wide asunder as any two things in the world; and what God has separated, let no man pretend to join. Indeed, the spirit of religion can have no fellowship with sloth, indolence, and self-indulgence. But still, a Christian does not carry on his common trade quite like another man neither; for something of the spirit which he labors to attain at church, he carries with him into his worldly concerns; while there are some who set up for Sunday Christians, who have no notion that they are bound to be week-day Christians too.

WILL. Why, master, I do think, if God Almighty is contented with one day in seven, he wont thank you for throwing him the other six into the bargain. I thought he gave us them for our own use; and I am sure nobody works harder all the week than you do.

STOCK. God, it is true, sets apart one day in seven for actual rest from labor, and for more immediate devotion to his service. But show me that text wherein he says, Thou shalt love the Lord thy God on *Sundays*; thou shalt keep my commandments on the *Sabbath-day*; to be carnally minded on *Sundays, is death*; cease to do evil, and learn to do well *one day in seven*; grow in grace on the *Lord's day*. Is there any such text?

WILL. No, to be sure there is not; for that would be encouraging sin on all the other days.

STOCK. Yes, just as you do when you make religion a thing for the church, and not for the world. There is no one lawful calling, in pursuing which we may not serve God acceptably. You and I may serve him while we are stitching this pair of boots; farmer Furrow, while he is plowing yonder field; Betsy Best, over the way, while she is nursing her sick mother; neighbor Incle, in measuring out his tapes and ribbons. I say, all these may serve God just as acceptably in those employments as at church; I had almost said more so.

WILL. Aye, indeed; how can that be? Now, you're too much on t'other side.

STOCK. Because a man's trials in trade being often greater, they give him fresh means of glorifying God, and proving the sincerity of religion. A man who mixes in business, is naturally brought into continual temptations and difficulties. These will lead him, if he be a good man, to look more to God than he perhaps would otherwise do. He sees temptations on the right hand and on the left; he knows that there are snares all around him, this makes him watchful: he feels that the enemy within is too ready to betray him, this makes him humble himself; while a sense of his own difficulties makes him tender to the failings of others.

WILL. Then you would make one believe, after all, that trade and business must be sinful in itself, since it brings a man into all these snares and scrapes.

STOCK. No, no, Will; trade and business don't create evil passions—they were in the heart before, only now and then they seem to lie snug a little; our concerns with the world bring them out into action a little more, and thus show both others and ourselves what we really are. But then, as the world offers more trials on the one hand, so on the other it holds out more duties. If we are called to battle oftener, we have more opportunities of victory. Every temptation resisted, is an enemy subdued; and "he that ruleth his own spirit, is better than he that taketh a city."[1]

WILL. I don't quite understand you, master.

STOCK. I will try to explain myself. There is no passion more called out by the transactions of trade than covetousness. Now, 'tis impossible to withstand such a master-sin as that, without carrying a good deal of the spirit of religion into one's trade.

WILL. Well, I own I don't yet see how I am to be religious when I am hard at work, or busy settling an account. I can't do two things at once; 'tis as if I were to pretend to make a shoe and cut out a boot at the same moment.

---

1 Proverbs 16:32—He that is slow to anger is better than the mighty; and he that ruleth his spirit than he that taketh a city.

STOCK. I tell you, both must subsist together. Nay, the one must be the motive to the other. God commands us to be industrious; and if we love him, the desire of pleasing him should be the main-spring of our industry.

WILL. I don't see how I can always be thinking about pleasing God.

STOCK. Suppose, now, a man had a wife and children whom he loved and wished to serve, would not he be often thinking about them while he was at work? and though he should not be *always* thinking about them, yet would not the very love he bore them be a constant spur to his industry? He would always be pursuing the same course from the same motive, though his words, and even his thoughts, must often be taken up in the common transactions of life.

WILL. Well, I say first one, then the other; now for labor, now for religion.

STOCK. I will show that both must go together. I will suppose you were going to buy so many skins of our currier: that is quite a worldly transaction—you can't see what a spirit of religion has to do with buying a few calfskins. Now, I tell you it has a great deal to do with it. Covetousness, a desire to make a good bargain, may rise up in your heart. Selfishness, a spirit of monopoly, a wish to get all, in order to distress others—these are evil desires, and must be subdued. Some opportunity of unfair gain offers, in which there may be much sin, and yet little scandal. Here a Christian will stop short; he will recollect, that "he who maketh haste to be rich shall hardly be innocent."[1]

Perhaps the sin may be on the side of your dealer: he may want to overreach you—this is provoking; you are tempted to violent anger, perhaps to swear—here is a fresh demand on you for a spirit of patience and moderation, as there was before for a spirit of justice and self-denial. If, by God's grace, you get the victory over these temptations, you are the better man for having been called out to them; always provided, that the temptations be not of your own seeking. If you give way, and sink under these temptations, don't go and say that trade and business have made you covetous, passionate, and profane. No, no; depend upon it, you were so before: you would have had all these evil seeds lurking in your heart, if you had been loitering about at home, and doing nothing, with the additional sin of idleness into the bargain. When you are busy, the devil often tempts you; when you are idle, you tempt the devil. If business and the world call these evil tempers into action, business and the world call that religion into action too, which teaches us to resist them. And in this you see the week-day fruit of the Sunday's piety. 'Tis trade and business in the week which calls us to put our Sunday readings, praying, and church-going into practice.

WILL. Well, master, you have a comical way,

1 Proverbs 28:20—A faithful man shall abound with blessings: but he that maketh haste to be rich shall not be innocent.

somehow, of coming over one. I never should have thought there would have been any religion wanted in buying and selling a few calf-skins. But I begin to see there is a good deal in what you say. And whenever I am doing a common action, I will try to remember that it must be done *after a godly sort.*

STOCK. I hear the clock strike nine—let us leave off our work. I will only observe farther, that one good end of our bringing religion into our business is, to put us in mind not to undertake more business than we can carry on consistently with our religion. I shall never commend that man's diligence, though it is often commended by the world, who is not diligent about the salvation of his soul. We are as much forbidden to be overcharged with the *cares* of life as with its *pleasures.* I only wish to prove to you, that a discreet Christian may be wise for both worlds; that he may employ his hands without entangling his soul, and labor for the meat that perisheth without neglecting that which endureth unto eternal life; that he may be prudent for time, while he is wise for eternity.

PART VI

DIALOGUE THE SECOND.

ON THE DUTY OF CARRYING RELIGION INTO OUR AMUSEMENTS

THE next evening, Will Simpson being got first to his work, Mr. Stock found him singing very cheerfully over his last. His master's entrance did not prevent his finishing his song, which concluded with these words:—

"Since life is no more than a passage at best,
Let us strew the way over with flowers."

When Will had concluded his song, he turned to Mr. Stock, and said, "I thank you, master, for first putting it into my head how wicked it is to sing profane and indecent songs. I never sing any now which have any wicked words in them."

STOCK. I am glad to hear it. So far you do well. But there are other things as bad as wicked words; nay, worse perhaps, though they do not so much shock the ear of decency.

WILL. What is that, master? What *can* be so bad as wicked words?

STOCK. Wicked *thoughts*, Will. Which thoughts, when they are covered over with smooth words, and dressed out in pleasing rhymes, so as not to shock modest young people by the sound, do more harm to their principles than those songs of which the words are so gross and disgusting, that no person of common decency can for a moment listen to them.

WILL. Well, master, I am sure that was a very pretty song I was singing when you came in, and a song which very sober, good people sing.

STOCK. Do they? Then I will be bold to say, that singing such songs is no part of their goodness. I heard indeed but two lines of it, but they were so heathenish that I desire to hear no more.

WILL. Now you are really too hard. What harm could there be in it? there was not one indecent word.

STOCK. I own, indeed, that indecent words are particularly offensive. But, as I said before, though immodest expressions offend the ear more, they do not corrupt the heart, perhaps, much more than songs of which the words are decent, and the principles vicious. In the latter case, because there is nothing that shocks his ear, a man listens till the sentiment has so corrupted his heart, that his ear grows hardened to, and by long custom he loses all sense of the danger of profane diversions; and I must say I have often heard young women of character sing songs in company, which I should be ashamed to read by myself. But come, as we work, let us talk over this business a little; and first let us stick to this sober song of yours that you boast so much about. (*Repeats.*)

> *"Since life is no more than a passage at best,*
> *Let us strew the way over with flowers."*

Now, what do you learn by this?

WILL. Why, master, I don't pretend to learn much by it. But 'tis a pretty tune and pretty words.

STOCK. But what do those pretty words mean?

WILL. That we must make ourselves merry, because life is short.

STOCK. Will! Of what religion are you?

WILL. You are always asking one such odd questions, master: why, a Christian, to be sure.

STOCK. If I often ask you, or others, this question, it is only because I like to know what grounds I am to go upon when I am talking with you or them. I conceive that there are in this country two sorts of people—Christians, and no Christians. Now, if people profess to be of this first description, I expect one kind of notions, opinions, and behavior from them; if they say they are of the latter, then I look for another set of notions and actions from them. I compel no man to think with me. I take every man at his word. I only expect him to think and believe according to the character he takes upon himself, and to act on the principles of that character which he professes to maintain.

WILL. That's fair enough—I can't say but it is—to take a man at his own word, and on his own grounds.

STOCK. Well, then. Of whom does the Scripture speak, when it says, "Let us eat and drink, for tomorrow we die?"[1]

WILL. Why, of heathens, to be sure; not of Christians.

STOCK. And of whom, when it says, "Let us crown ourselves with rosebuds before they are withered?"[2]

Will. O, that is Solomon's worldly fool.

STOCK. You disapprove of both, then?

WILL. To be sure I do. I should not be a Christian if I did not.

STOCK. And yet, though a Christian, you are admiring the very same thought in the song you were singing. How do you reconcile this?

WILL. O, there is no comparison between them. These several texts are designed to describe loose, wicked heathens. Now, I learn texts as part of my religion. But religion, you know, has nothing to do with a song. I sing a song for my pleasure.

STOCK. In our last night's talk, Will, I endeavored to prove to you that religion was to be brought into our *business*. I wish now to let you see that it is to be brought into our *pleasure* also; and that he who is really a Christian,

---

1 1 Corintians 15:32–33—If after the manner of men I have fought with beasts at Ephesus, what advantageth it me, if the dead rise not? let us eat and drink; for tomorrow we die. Be not deceived: evil communications corrupt good manners.

2 Book of Wisdom 2:8.

must be a Christian in his very diversions.

WILL. Now you are too strict again, master; as you last night declared, that in our business you would not have us always praying, so I hope that in our pleasure you would not have us always psalm-singing. I hope you would not have all one's singing to be about good things?

STOCK. Not so, Will; but I would not have any part, either of our business or our pleasure, to be about evil things. It is one thing to be singing *about* religion, it is another thing to be singing *against* it. Saint Peter, I fancy, would not much have approved your favorite song. He, at least, seemed to have another view of the matter, when he said, "The end of all things is at hand."[1] Now, this text teaches much the same awful truth with the first line of your song. But let us see to what different purposes the apostle and the poet turn the very same thought. Your song says, because life is so short, let us make it merry. Let us divert ourselves so much on the road, that we may forget the end. Now, what says the apostle? "Because the end of all things is at hand, be ye therefore sober, and watch unto prayer."

WILL. Why, master, I like to be sober too, and have left off drinking. But still, I never thought that we were obliged to carry texts out of the Bible to try the soundness of a song, and to enable us to judge if we might be both merry and wise in singing it.

---

1 1 Peter 4:7—But the end of all things is at hand: be ye therefore sober, and watch unto prayer.

STOCK. Providence has not so stinted our enjoyments, Will, but he has left us many subjects of harmless merriment: but, for my own part, I am never certain that any one is quite harmless till I have tried it by this rule that you seem to think so strict. There is another favorite catch which I heard you and some of the workmen humming yesterday.

WILL. I will prove to you that there is not a word of harm in *that:* pray listen now. (*Sings.*)

"Which is the properest day to drink—
Sunday, Monday, Tuesday,
Wednesday, Thursday, Friday, Saturday?"

STOCK. Now, Will, do you really find your unwillingness to drink is so great, that you stand in need of all these incentives to provoke you to it? do you not find temptation strong enough, without exciting your inclinations, and whetting your appetites in this manner? can any thing be more unchristian than to persuade youth, by pleasant words, set to the most alluring music, that the pleasures of drinking are so great, that every day in the week, naming them all successively, by way of fixing and enlarging the idea, is equally fit, equally proper, and equally delightful; for what?—for the low and sensual purpose of getting drunk. Tell me, Will, are you so very averse to pleasure? Are you naturally so cold and dead to all passion and temptation, that you really find it necessary to inflame your imagination, and disorder your senses, in order to excite a quicker relish for the pleasures of sin?

WILL. All this is true enough, indeed; but I never saw it in this light before.

STOCK. As I passed by the Greyhound last night, in the way to my evening's walk in the fields, I caught this one verse of a song which the club were singing:—

"Bring the flask, the music bring,
Joy shall quickly find us;
Drink and dance, and laugh and sing,
And cast dull care behind us."

When I got into the fields, I could not forbear comparing this song with the second lesson last Sunday evening at church; these were the words:—"Take heed, lest at any time your heart be overcharged with drunkenness, and so that day come upon you unawares, for as a snare shall it come upon all them that are on the face of the earth."[1]

WILL. Why, to be sure, if the second lesson was right, the song must be wrong.

STOCK. I ran over in my mind also a comparison between such songs as that which begins with

"Drink, and drive care away,"

with those injunctions of holy writ, "Watch and pray, therefore, that you enter not into temptation;"[2] and again, "Watch and pray, that

1 Luke 21:34–35—And take heed to yourselves, lest at any time your hearts be overcharged with surfeiting, and drunkenness, and cares of this life, and so that day come upon you unawares. For as a snare shall it come on all them that dwell on the face of the whole earth.

2 Matthew 26:41—Watch and pray, that ye enter not into temptation: the spirit indeed is willing, but the flesh is weak.

you may escape all these things." I say, I compared this with the song I allude to,

"Drink and drive care away,
Drink and be merry;
You'll ne'er go the faster
To the Stygian ferry."

I compared this with that awful admonition of Scripture how to pass the time, "not in rioting and drunkenness, not in chambering and wantonness; but put ye on the Lord Jesus Christ, and make not provision for the flesh, to fulfill the lusts thereof."[1]

WILL. I am afraid, then, master, you would not much approve of what I used to think a very pretty song, which begins with,

"A plague on those musty old lubbers,
Who teach us to fast and to think."

STOCK. Will, what would you think of any one who should sit down and write a book or a song to abuse the clergy?

WILL. Why, I should think he was a very wicked fellow, and I hope no one would look into such a book, or sing such a song.

STOCK. And yet it must certainly be the clergy who are scoffed at in that verse, it being their professed business to teach us to think and be serious.

WILL. Ay, master, and now you have opened

1 Romans 13:14—But put ye on the Lord Jesus Christ, and make not provision for the flesh, to fulfil the lusts thereof.

my eyes, I think I can make some of those comparisons myself between the spirit of the Bible and the spirit of these songs.

"Bring the flask, the goblet bring"

won't stand very well in company with the threat of the prophet, "Woe unto them that rise up early, that they may mingle strong drink."[1]

STOCK. Ay, Will; and these thoughtless people who live up to their singing, seem to be the very people described in another place as glorying in their intemperance, and acting what their songs describe—"They look at the wine, and say it is red, it moveth itself aright in the cup."[2]

WILL. I do hope I shall for the future not only become more careful what songs I sing myself, but also, not to keep company with those who sing nothing else but what, in my sober judgment, I now see to be wrong.

STOCK. As we shall have no *body* in the world to come, it is a pity not only to make our pleasures here consist entirely in the delights of animal life, but to make our very songs consist in extolling and exalting those delights which are unworthy of the man as well as of the Christian. If, through temptation or weakness, we fall into errors, let us not establish and confirm them, by picking up all the songs and scraps of verses which excuse, justify, and commend sin. That

1 Isaiah 5:22—Woe unto them that are mighty to drink wine, and men of strength to mingle strong drink.

2 Proverbs 23:31—Look not thou upon the wine when it is red, when it giveth his colour in the cup, when it moveth itself aright.

"time is short," is a reason given by these songmongers why we should give into greater indulgences. That "time is short," is a reason given by the apostle why we should enjoy our dearest comforts as if we enjoyed them not.

Now, Will, I hope you will see the importance of so managing, that our diversions (for diversions of some kind we all require) may be as carefully chosen as our other employments. For to make them such as shall effectually drive out of our minds all that the Bible and the minister have been putting into them, seems to me as imprudent as it is unchristian. But this is not all. Such sentiments as these songs contain, set off by the prettiest music, heightened by liquor, and all the noise and spirit of what is called jovial company; all this, I say, not only puts every thing that is right out of the mind, but puts every thing that is wrong into it. Such songs, therefore, as tend to promote levity, thoughtlessness, loose imaginations, false views of life, forgetfulness of death, contempt of whatever is serious, and neglect of whatever is sober, whether they be love-songs or drinking-songs, will not, cannot be sung by any man or any woman who makes a serious profession of Christianity.[1]

[The popular author and singer here alluded to, was the late Charles Dibdin, who obtained a pension of

1 It is with regret I have lately observed, that the fashionable author and singer of songs more loose, profane, and corrupt than any of those here noticed, not only received a prize as the reward of his important services, but received also the public acknowledgments of an illustrious society, for having *contributed to the happiness of their country!*

£200 a year, from government, during the administration of Mr. Pitt, as a reward for his loyal ballads, which certainly had a wonderful effect, especially in the navy. When Mr. Pitt died, however, the pension was withdrawn, and poor Dibdin ended his days in poverty.]

O THAT THE LORD WOULD GUIDE MY WAYS

O that the Lord would guide my ways,
To keep his statutes still;
O that my God would give me grace
To know and do his will.

Lord, send thy Spirit down to write
Thy love upon my heart;
Nor let my tongue indulge deceit,
Nor act a liar's part.

From vanity turn off mine eyes;
Let no corrupt design,
Nor covetous desires arise
Within this soul of mine.

Order my footsteps by thy word,
And make my heart sincere;
Let sin have no dominion, Lord,
But keep my conscience clear.

My soul hath gone too far astray,
My feet too often slip;
I would not, Lord, forget thy way,
Bring back thy wandering sheep.

Make me to walk in thy commands,
'Tis a delightful road;
Nor let my head, or heart, or hands,
Offend against my God. —Isaac Watts

www.ingramcontent.com/pod-product-compliance
Lightning Source LLC
LaVergne TN
LVHW051011080826
845145LV00009B/2571

9781935626053